Christmas
STORIES

Christmas STORIES

*Heartwarming Classics
of Angels, a Manger, and
the Birth of Hope*

MAX LUCADO

THOMAS NELSON
Since 1798

Christmas Stories

The Christmas Child © 2003 by Max Lucado, previously published as *The Christmas Cross*
Jacob's Gift © 1998 by Max Lucado
The Christmas Candle © 2006 by Max Lucado
An Angel's Story © 2002, 2004 by Max Lucado, previously published as *Cosmic Christmas*

Published in Nashville, Tennessee, by Thomas Nelson. Thomas Nelson is a registered trademark of HarperCollins Christian Publishing, Inc.

Thomas Nelson titles may be purchased in bulk for educational, business, fundraising, or sales promotional use. For information, please e-mail SpecialMarkets@ThomasNelson.com.

An Angel's Story is based in part on a story by David Lambert entitled "Earthward, Earthward, Messenger Bright," which first appeared in the December 1982 issue of *Moody Monthly*. "Earthward, Earthward, Messenger Bright" © 1982, 1990 by David Lambert.

Scripture quotations marked KJV are taken from the King James Version. Public domain. Scripture quotations marked NIV are taken from The Holy Bible, New International Version®, NIV®. Copyright © 1973, 1978, 1984, 2011 by Biblica, Inc.® Used by permission of Zondervan. All rights reserved worldwide. www.Zondervan.com. The "NIV" and "New International Version" are trademarks registered in the United States Patent and Trademark Office by Biblica, Inc.® Scripture quotations marked NKJV are taken from the New King James Version®. Copyright © 1982 by Thomas Nelson. Used by permission. All rights reserved. Scripture quotations marked MSG are taken from THE MESSAGE. Copyright © 1993, 2002, 2018 by Eugene H. Peterson. Used by permission of NavPress. All rights reserved. Represented by Tyndale House Publishers, a Division of Tyndale House Ministries. Scripture quotations marked NASB are taken from the New American Standard Bible® (NASB). Copyright © 1960, 1962, 1963, 1968, 1971, 1972, 1973, 1975, 1977, 1995 by The Lockman Foundation. Used by permission. www.Lockman.org. Scripture quotations marked NCV are taken from the New Century Version®. Copyright © 2005 by Thomas Nelson. Used by permission. All rights reserved. Scripture quotations marked NLT are taken from the Holy Bible, New Living Translation. Copyright © 1996, 2004, 2015 by Tyndale House Foundation. Used by permission of Tyndale House Ministries, Carol Stream, Illinois 60188. All rights reserved.

ISBN 978-1-4016-8543-0 (hardcover)
ISBN 978-1-4016-8544-7 (e-book)
ISBN 978-0-7852-4965-8 (repack)

Library of Congress Cataloging-in-Publication Data

CIP data is available upon request.

Printed in the United States of America

22 23 24 25 LSC 10 9 8 7 6 5 4 3

For Dr. Jim Martin. While there is only one Great Physician, you come as close as any doc I know. Thanks for bringing health and hope to thousands of families—especially mine.

CONTENTS

Contents

CHRIST IS BORN

MERRY CHRISTMAS,
DEAR READER

Dear Reader,

Along with the sights and sounds of Christmas, there's something about this season that makes us yearn for stories, doesn't it? Stories that take us back to the meaning of the coming Savior, the hope of heaven.

My hope is that this new edition of *Christmas Stories*

will be just the reminder you need. It includes three main stories about a burnt-out candlemaker, a lonely businessman, and heavenly angels, as well as other pieces interspersed throughout—each one crafted to point to the reason for this season.

In the hustle and bustle that often distracts us at this time of year, my prayer is that these stories will help you explore the ways Christ's coming has forever changed history—and you. Because the promise of Christmas is personal. God's promise for you and me. Whether you've read these stories over and over, or you're discovering them for the first time, hang on to that promise of hope.

So, find a cozy chair, grab a snowman cookie and a mug of hot chocolate. And turn the page.

THE FIRST
CHRISTMAS GIFT

*T*he world was different this week. It was temporarily transformed.

The magical dust of Christmas glittered on the cheeks of humanity ever so briefly, reminding us of what is worth having and what we were intended to be.

We forgot our compulsion with winning, wooing, and warring. We put away our ladders and ledgers; we hung up our stopwatches and weapons. We stepped off our race tracks and roller coasters and looked outward toward the star of Bethlehem.

We reminded ourselves that Jesus came as a babe, born in a manger.

I'd like to suggest that we remind ourselves he still comes.

He comes to those as small as Mary's baby and as poor as a carpenter's boy.

He comes to those as young as a Nazarene teenager and as forgotten as an unnoticed kid in an obscure village.

He comes to those as busy as the oldest son of a large family, to those as stressed as the leader of restless disciples, to those as tired as one with no pillow for his head.

He comes and gives us the gift of himself.

Sunsets steal our breath. Caribbean blue stills our hearts. Newborn babies stir our tears. Lifelong love bejewels our lives. But take all these away—strip away the sunsets, oceans, cooing babies, and tender hearts— and leave us in the Sahara, and we still have reason to dance in the sand. Why? Because God is with us.

He comes to all. He speaks to all. Let's let him speak to us this Christmas.

Christ Is Celebrated

*W*hen you give a word of
kindness to someone who needs
it, that's an act of worship.

—MAX LUCADO

The Christmas Candle

*C*hristmas celebrates a coming. An arrival. An advent. Christmas remembers God showing up. Not showing off with angel-driven chariots or Magic Kingdom fireworks. But showing up on a donkey, with a carpenter in the belly of a peasant girl. Christmas commemorates God's most uncommon decision: to come commonly.

And Christmas wonders if he still does. If he shows up amidst the regular folk in the sleepy moments of life. This story, "The Christmas Candle," welcomes such wonderings. If he came to Bethlehem, might he not come to Gladstone, England? And, if he touched the world of a carpenter, wouldn't he touch the world of a candlemaker? I think so.

Even more, he would touch our world too.

THE ANGEL'S
TOUCH

December 1664

Light exploded in the small house, making midnight seem as daylight. The bearded candlemaker and his wife popped up in bed.

"Wh-wh-what is it?" she asked, trembling.

"Don't move!"

"But the children?"

"They're sleeping. Stay where you are!"

The wife pulled the blanket up to her chin and took a quick look around the shadowless room: children asleep on the floor, the table and chairs resting near the hearth, tools piled in the corner.

The candlemaker never shifted his wide-eyed gaze. The figure wore a singular flame: a heatless tongue stretching from ceiling to floor. His form moved within the blaze: a torso, head, and two arms. He reached out of the radiance and extended a finger toward a rack of hanging candles. When he did, the couple squeezed together and slid farther back in the bed.

The husband mustered a question: "Are you going to hurt us?"

The visitor gave no reply. He waited, as if to ensure the couple was watching, touched one of the candles, and then vanished.

The room darkened, and the just-touched candle glowed. The man instinctively reached for it, stepping quickly out of bed and across the room, grabbing the candle just as the light diminished.

He looked at his wife. She gulped.

"What just happened?" she asked.

"I don't know."

He moved to the table and sat. She hurried to do the same.

"An angel?" she wondered aloud.

"Must be."

He placed the candle on the table, and both stared at it. Neither knew what to say or to think.

The next morning found them still sitting. Still staring.

Their children awoke, so they ate breakfast, dressed warmly, and walked the half mile up Bristol Lane to St. Mark's Church for the celebration of the final Sunday of Advent. The candlemaker gave the rector extra candles for the Advent service but kept the angel-touched candle in his coat pocket. He started to mention the visitation to the reverend but stopped short. *He won't believe me.*

The couple tried to concentrate on the sermon but couldn't. Their minds kept reliving the light, the angel, and the glowing candle.

They shared a pew with a young mother and her

two children, all three disheveled and dirty. The couple knew her, knew how her husband, a servant to a baron, had died a month before in a hunt.

After the service, the widow described her plight to them. "We have little food left. Enough for a few days."

The chandler's wife reached into her husband's coat pocket for a coin. When she did, she felt the candle. She handed both to the young mother, inviting, "Light this and pray." As the young mother turned to leave, the wife looked at her husband and shrugged as if to say, "What harm?"

He nodded.

They spoke some about the candle over the next few days but not much. Both were willing to dismiss it as a dream, perhaps a vision.

The Christmas Eve service changed that. It began with a time of blessing-sharing. Anyone in the congregation who wanted to give public thanks to God could do so. When the rector asked for volunteers, the young mother stood up. The same woman who, days earlier, had appeared unkempt and hungry. This night she beamed. She told the congregation how a wealthy uncle in a nearby county had given her a farm as a gift. The farm was a godsend. She could live in the house and lease the land and support her family. She looked straight at the candlemaker and his wife as she said, "I prayed. I lit the candle and prayed."

The couple looked at each other. They suspected a connection between the candle and the answered prayer, but who knew for sure?

Chapter 1

AFTERNOON

May 4, 1864

I just think it odd that Oxford would assign its top student to a village like Gladstone," Edward Haddington said to his wife, Bea. A broad-shouldered man with a brilliant set of dark eyes and full gray eyebrows, he wrestled to button the waistcoat over his rotund belly.

Equally plump Bea was having troubles of her own. "How long since I wore this dress?" she wondered aloud.

"Must I let it out again?" Then louder, "Edward, hurry. He's due within the hour."

"Don't you think it odd?"

"I don't know what to think, dear. But I know we need to leave now if we don't want to be late. He arrives at half past one."

The couple hurried out of the small, gabled house and scurried the half mile south on Bristol Lane toward the center of the village. They weren't alone. A dozen or more villagers walked ahead of them. By the time Edward and Bea reached the town commons, at least half the citizens of Gladstone, some sixty people, stood staring northward. No one noticed the white-haired couple. All eyes were on the inbound wagon.

The driver pulled the horses to a halt, and a young man stood to exit. He bore beady eyes, a pointed chin, and his angular nose seemed to descend forever before finding a place to stop. With a tall hat in his hand and a black coat draped on his shoulders, Rev. David Richmond surveyed the crowd. Edward detected a sigh.

"We must appear odd to him," he whispered to Bea. She cupped an ear toward him. "What?"

He shook his head, not wanting to risk being overheard.

A goggle-eyed locksmith, so humped from filing he had to greet the guest with a sideways, upward glance, extended the first hello. Next came a short farmer and his Herculean, simpleminded son. "He can clean the windows in the church," the father offered. "He did for Reverend Pillington." A mill worker asked Reverend Richmond if he liked to fish. Before he could reply, a laborer invited the minister to join him and his friends at the pub.

"Let the man breathe, dear people. Let him breathe." The citizens parted to let Edward extend his hand. "A fine welcome to Gladstone, Reverend. Did you enjoy the carriage ride?"

Reverend Richmond had ample reason to say yes. Spring had decked the Cotswolds in her finest fashions. Waist-high stone walls framed the fields. Puffy flocks dotted the pastures. Crows scavenged seeds from melting snow. May clouds passed and parted, permitting sunlight to glint off the shallow creeks. England at her best. Yet the minister replied with an unconvincing, "It was pleasant."

Edward picked up the clergyman's bag and led him through the crowd. "We'll deposit your things at the parsonage and let you freshen up. Then I'll leave you with the Barstow family for tea."

As the crowd dispersed, the reverend nodded and followed his hosts toward the manse. It sat in the shadow of St. Mark's Church, which was only a stone's throw from the center of town. The hoary, dog-toothed Norman tower stood guard over the village. Edward paused in front of the church gate and invited, "Would you like to take a look inside?"

The guest nodded, and the three entered the grounds.

A cemetery separated the church from the road. "To preach to the living, you have to pass through the dead," Edward quipped.

"Edward!" Bea corrected.

Reverend Richmond offered no reply.

The walls of the path through the cemetery were, at points, shoulder high, elevating the headstones to eye level. The newest one lay beneath the tallest yew tree near the church entrance and marked the burial place of

St. Mark's former rector. Edward and Bea paused, giving Richmond time to read the inscription:

REVEREND P. PILLINGTON
Man of God.
Man of Faith.
Man of Gladstone.
Ours, but for a moment.
God's forever.
1789–1864

"This month we'd have celebrated his fiftieth year at the church," said Bea.

"When did he die?" the reverend asked.

"February," Edward answered. "Hard winter. Pneumonia took him."

"God took him," Bea altered.

Edward nodded. "We dearly loved the man. You'll find his fingerprints throughout the valley. He taught us to trust, to pray. He even taught me to read and write."

Bea chimed in. "Edward here was a diligent student. Come ahead. Let's step inside."

The heavy doors opened to the rear of the sanctuary. Three shafts of stained-glass sunlight spilled through tall windows. "My grandfather helped install those," Edward offered. He strode the five short steps to the baptismal font and motioned for the reverend to join him. "Dates back two centuries," Edward said, running a finger along the limestone. "My ancestors were all baptized here. In fact, my great-great—Bea, how many 'greats' is it?"

She placed a finger to her lips. "Let the reverend meditate."

Edward apologized with a wave and stepped back.

One aisle separated two groups of ten pews. A lectern faced the seats on the left, and a pulpit presided over the church from the right. Brass organ pipes climbed the chancel wall behind the pulpit, where two sets of choir benches faced each other.

"My Bea plays the organ," Edward boasted.

The clergyman didn't respond. He made the short walk to the front and stopped at the first of the five swaybacked stone steps leading up to the pulpit. A thick Bible and empty glass rested on the stand.

"Been vacant since February," Edward offered.

Reverend Richmond turned with a puzzled look. "No minister filled in?"

Bea shook her head. "Only on occasion. Gladstone is too remote for most clergymen. But we've gotten by."

"Right," Reverend Richmond said, suddenly ready to leave. "Shall we move on?"

Bea extended a hand. "I'll go home and prepare some dinner. Reverend, enjoy your visit to Gladstone."

Edward showed the minister the parsonage and waited outside until he was ready for the first appointment of the afternoon.

Charles Barstow cut an imposing figure standing in his doorway: thick shoulders, long face, hollow cheeks flanked by snow-white sideburns, and eyebrows as thick as hedges.

As Edward presented the reverend, he explained, "Charles runs the local mercantile. Need boots, hats, or hammers? He can help you."

Richmond noted the fine house: ivy framed its dormers; jasmine and roses charmed the porch.

"Charles, I'll leave him in your care," Edward said. "Fine."

Mr. Barstow's wife joined him at the door and

escorted them to a table in the inglenook next to the fireplace. She stood much shorter than the two men, her head level with her husband's shoulders. She was overdressed, better attired for the theatre than for tea. She attempted a sophisticated air, as if wanting to be in, or at least from, some other town. "Tell me," she nasaled, pausing after each word. "How is life in Oxford?"

Her husband sighed and motioned for the minister to sit. "I understand you grew up in London."

"I did."

"My family is from Putney—some time back, however. And yours?"

"Kensington. I'm the first to leave the city, actually. That is, if I do. I shall be the first in our family not to serve the royal household in generations."

"Oh." Mrs. Barstow perked up. "What is your connection?"

"My father is a barrister."

"My, my," Mrs. Barstow admired.

The Barstows' granddaughter, Emily, joined them at the table.

Reverend Richmond was grateful to see someone

closer to his age, even more thankful to see someone so pretty. Emily's curled brown locks fell to her shoulders. Her warm hazel eyes ducked from his glance. He looked away, equally embarrassed.

"I hear you have no wife," her grandmother said.

Emily blushed. The reverend caught the hint but didn't reply.

Mr. Barstow redirected the conversation with questions about Oxford, but his wife was not easily deterred. At the next pause, she jumped in. "Our dear friend's niece will marry next week. As for us, we have no plans."

Emily, who still hadn't spoken, shot a glance at her grandmother.

"That's good to know," Reverend Richmond offered, then corrected himself. "I mean, it's nice that your friend is marrying, and, well, I hope you will . . . or your granddaughter will marry soon as well. If she wants to, that is."

"Tell me, Reverend." Charles spoke, to the minister's relief. "What do you think of the candle?"

"The candle?"

"The Gladstone Candle."

"I, uh, can't say I've heard of it."

The three Barstows shared wide-eyed glances.

"You've never heard of the candle?" Mrs. Barstow asked.

"Or the candlemaker?" Mr. Barstow added.

"Or the Christmas miracles?" Emily completed.

"No," the reverend admitted, feeling that he'd missed a long conversation.

The three looked at him with eyes reserved for a sumptuous meal, each wanting to eat first. "Well, let me tell you—" Mrs. Barstow volunteered.

"Maybe I should do that," her husband interrupted. But a knock at the door stopped him. He stood and answered it.

"I knew if I didn't come, you'd forget to bring him to our house," said a friendly, round-faced woman.

Mr. Barstow turned toward the minister.

"This is Sarah Chumley. She'll take you to your next visit."

Reverend Richmond gave her a puzzled look. Sarah chuckled. "You've apparently met my twin, Bea Haddington. Don't even try to tell us apart. People who have known us for years still grow confused."

Richmond stood, thanking his guests. Mrs. Barstow

spoke again. "I'll be glad to finish what we started, Reverend."

Did she mean the candle or the courting? He didn't know and didn't dare ask. He turned and smiled a half smile, grateful to be leaving.

Sarah Chumley was as cheerful as the morning sun, was wide-waisted, and blessed with plump cheeks that flushed with rose and rendered eyes into half moons at the slightest smile. She escorted the minister down the street, two houses past St. Mark's Church. She paused at the parsonage that separated her home from the church building. "This is the—"

"I know, the parsonage. I've already dropped off my bags."

"Reverend Pillington lived here for half a century. A dear man. Scratchy after souls, he was." She paused as if enjoying a memory, then invited, "Come. Mr. Chumley looks forward to meeting you."

She led Reverend Richmond through a chest-high gate and a golden garden of goldilocks and buttercups. Wisteria stretched over the honey-colored cottage walls, and bright red paint accented the front door. Her husband opened it, not to let them in, but to let a patient out.

"Keep it wrapped, now, Mr. Kendall. Apply the liniment like I showed you, and"—placing a hand on the old man's shoulders, Mr. Chumley winked—"Don't you think it's time you let the younger people birth the lambs?"

"I'm as spry as I ever was," the man countered.

"Hello, madam," he added.

"Afternoon," Sarah greeted. She and the reverend stepped aside so the injured shepherd could pass. "My husband's the village alchemist, closest thing Gladstone has to a doctor. Try to find a villager he hasn't treated—you won't find one."

Mr. Chumley was a slight man, bespectacled and short. But for a crown of gray, he would have been bald. "Come in, come in!" He clasped his hands together. "Been looking forward to meeting you." He led them through the pharmacy in the front of the house to the parlor, where the reverend entered into his second conversation of the afternoon. He soon discovered that Mr. Chumley and the former rector had been fast friends. The two men had shared tea, problems, and long winters; but, curiously, they hadn't shared matters of faith. "I leave things of God with God," Mr. Chumley stated pointedly.

"I can respect that," Reverend Richmond said.

"You can?"

"Of course I can. Theology has changed since your former rector studied."

The reverend noted Sarah's furrowed brow but continued. "God keeps his distance, you know. He steps in with Red Sea and resurrection moments, but most of the time he leaves living life up to us."

"I've never heard such thoughts," Sarah said, joining the two men at the table.

"Nor have I, but I've had them," Mr. Chumley agreed. "I treat the body and leave the treatment of the soul to those who believe one exists." He reached across the table and placed a hand on Sarah's. "Like my wife."

"I still pray for him, however."

"And I still attend services . . . though my mind does wander."

The Chumley visit proved to be Reverend Richmond's most enjoyable of the day. He had dabbled in chemistry, and Mr. Chumley enjoyed debating theology. They took turns on each subject until the peal of St. Mark's tower clock prompted Sarah to interrupt. "I promised Bea to have you at their house within the hour."

"I'll take him," Mr. Chumley volunteered. He

donned a hat and grabbed his cane as the minister expressed thanks to his hostess, and the two stepped outside onto Bristol Lane, where horse hooves clicked on egg-shaped cobblestones, small thatched-roof houses lined the street, and villagers gave generous greetings.

"Good day, Mr. Chumley, Reverend," offered a seamstress carrying yards of cloth.

"Hello there, Mr. Chumley," saluted a farmer with mud-laden boots. "Those Epsom salts are helping the missus right well. Reverend, good to see you."

As they passed the town commons and the center cross, Mr. Chumley spoke about his in-laws, Bea and Edward Haddington. "The village treasures them. Not just because of the candle, mind you. They are dear, dear folk."

"What is this candle?" Reverend Richmond asked. "Mr. Barstow mentioned it to me as well."

The question stopped Mr. Chumley in his tracks. "You don't know about the candle?"

"No."

He removed his hat and scratched his head. "It's best that I let Edward tell you about it."

"And why is that?"

"He's the candlemaker."

Chapter 2

EVENING

May 4, 1864

Clad in his finest homespun Sunday coat, Edward Haddington was standing beneath the sign that read CHANDLER.

"He's all yours," Mr. Chumley said.

Edward smiled and reached up to wrap an arm around Reverend Richmond's shoulders. "Don't worry, my friend. We aren't eating in my shop. I was just checking a few matters."

Edward said good-bye to his brother-in-law and led

the minister next door, explaining as he walked, "My father and his father lived in the shop. I grew up there. But when I married, I promised Bea a house. She never could adjust to the smell of the candle shop. The tallow, you know. When her friends stopped coming over for tea . . . a change was needed." The two paused in front of the slate-roofed home.

"Our dwelling belonged to a tailor. When he died, his widow moved to Chaddington and sold it to us. What do you think?"

"Seems small." The reverend had to bend his neck to enter, lest he hit his head. The entire cottage consisted of one room. A table and four chairs sat to the right and a wrought-iron bed just beyond them. Two rockers rested in front of the fireplace, where a heating kettle filled the house with the smell of oxtail soup.

"Welcome to our home, Reverend. Won't you join us at the table?"

Reverend Richmond turned to see Bea, her silvered hair swept under a bonnet and glasses resting on her nose.

For the third time in one afternoon, the young man took a seat and began to eat. They drank beer and ate soup and just-baked bread.

Edward was never one for small talk. He went directly to his question. "How is it that you've come to Gladstone?"

"Excuse me?"

"Mr. Barstow says you excelled in your studies."

The reverend arched an eyebrow. "Well, yes, I did quite well."

"You seem awfully bright for our village. Seems you would be assigned to a, well, how would you say it, Bea . . . a more sophisticated parish? We're simple folk."

"Forgive us, Reverend," Bea interjected. "We don't mean to pry. We've never needed a new rector."

"Wouldn't you be better suited for a large church?" Edward persisted. "Perhaps in London? Don't you have family there?"

"No openings," was the reverend's terse reply.

Edward looked at Bea. She tilted her head as if to say, "Enough on this topic."

Edward looked away.

Bea proposed another question. "What do you find interesting about our village?"

Reverend Richmond stroked his beardless chin and remained silent. Edward got the impression that he was having a hard time coming up with anything. "The candle," he finally answered. "I'm curious about the candle."

Edward leaned forward. "Are you now? And what do you know about it?"

"Only that everyone keeps bringing it up."

"Are you sure you want to hear its history?" Bea asked.

"Why, of course."

"Perhaps we best fill our glasses, then."

As Bea poured, her husband lit his pipe and began to relate the details of Gladstone's favorite topic. "We need to go back a long way. I'm the seventh Haddington to make candles for Gladstone. The sign over the shop door? My grandfather made and hung it."

"Could use some paint," Bea added.

"My great-grandfather built the kiln. His great-grandfather, Papa Edward, migrated from Scandinavia in the 1650s. He built the shop and was the first Haddington to live in Gladstone. He was also the first to see the Christmas Candle."

"What do you mean, he *saw* the candle?" Reverend Richmond asked.

Bea spoke up. "We know less than we'd like about its origin. We'd know more had Edward's father not drowned in Evenlode River. It was a hard day, a hard time. Edward was sixteen, still an apprentice. He was not fully trained yet. A bit too young to run the shop, but what choice did he have?"

Edward shrugged. "Mother and I did the best we could. And, in time, we did fine. I married Bea and buried Mother, and Gladstone settled down to another generation of candle buying."

He leaned back in his chair and puffed on his pipe as though he'd finished the story. Indeed, he thought he had. Bea had to jog him. "Edward, tell him about the Christmas Candle."

"Oh, of course. Yes, well, as Bea said, some of the details died in the river along with my father. But what I and all of Gladstone know is this.

"Papa Edward had passed a bitterly cold Saturday evening dipping candles for the Sunday service. Being the night before the final Sunday in Christmas Advent, he'd made more than usual. To this day I still do. We stand them in the windowsills and give them to the choir to hold as they sing. We've always enjoyed yuletide services and large church crowds during December. Is it the same where you're from, Reverend? Why, I remember one year when Reverend Pillington arranged for a chorus from St. John's at Chadwick to join us. Bands of folks from three and four miles away came to sing the old, old songs."

He leaned forward and, with twinkling eyes and a bouncing head, sang a verse:

> *Peace and goodwill 'twixt rich and poor!*
> *Goodwill and peace 'twixt class and class!*
> *Let old with new, let Prince with boor*
> *Send round the bowl, and drain the glass!*

"Edward." Bea placed a hand on his. "The candle."

"Oh yes. The candle. Where were we?"

"The night before the final Sunday in Advent," Reverend Richmond aided.

"Right . . . Papa Edward and his wife were sound asleep when brightness exploded in the room. You would have thought a curtain had been yanked opened at noonday. A bonfire couldn't have been brighter. They sat up and saw a glowing angel. They watched him touch one of the candles and then disappear. Papa Edward grabbed it, looked at his wife, and the two spent the rest of the night wondering what had just happened."

"They had no idea what to think, Reverend," Bea continued. "They went to Sunday services saying nothing about the angel's visit. They feared people would think they were crazy. Before they left, however, Mrs. Haddington gave the candle away. Touched by the plight of a young widow, she gave her the candle and urged her to light it and pray."

Edward picked up the story. "Each Christmas Eve church members are invited to stand and share a blessing. Well, imagine who stood first that year?"

"The young woman?" asked the reverend.

"She was a changed person. A generous uncle had provided for her needs, and Grandmother and Grandfather Haddington wondered about a connection between the candle and the gift, but they drew no conclusion."

Edward took a drink from his glass. When he did, Bea spoke up. "Half by hope and half by obligation, they continued to hang extra candles each eve of the final Advent Sunday. Then, after a quarter of a century, the December night glowed, and an angel touched another candle. Papa Edward gave it to a shepherd who was searching for his son. The father found the son, shared the news at the Christmas Eve service, and Grandmother and Grandfather knew something special was happening."

The reverend shifted uneasily in his chair. "And you credit God for this?"

"Who else?" asked Edward.

"You realize, of course, that these could all be coincidences."

"Indeed they could," Edward conceded. "But two hundred years have passed. Every quarter of a century an angel has touched one candle. Every prayer that was offered over the candle was answered."

"The Christmas Candle has become legendary," Bea interjected, "and so have the Haddington candlemakers. Even when the region had other chandler shops, the angel only and always came to Papa Edward's descendants. The citizens of Gladstone have anticipated each candlemaker's child the way the rest of England awaits a royal heir, which brings us to the hard part of this story." She looked at Edward. "God gave us only one child, a son. He was born to us late in life and died from cholera when he was twenty."

"I'm sorry to hear that. Was he married?"

"That he was. His wife died several months later in childbirth."

"My goodness. One tragedy followed the other."

"It did. Indeed, it did."

Edward noted this first ray of warmth from the reverend. His guard, for just a few moments, was lowered.

"And your grandchild?" Richmond asked.

Edward chose to veil his reply. "As you can see, Bea and I are alone. We're both in our seventies; we won't be having any more children."

"Does that mean the angel visits stop with you?"

"We assume so."

Richmond began reviewing the facts, counting them with his fingers. "The angel comes once every twenty-five years?"

Edward nodded.

"He touches one candle?"

"So far."

"And that candle has power?"

"No, God has the power. The candle is just the . . . Bea, what did you call it?"

"The vessel."

"Yes, the vessel."

The young minister crossed his arms and looked out the window.

"You find the story hard to believe?" Bea asked.

Reverend Richmond cleared his throat and looked back. "It's not the type of event you hear about often."

"No," Edward agreed, "far from it."

"How long since the last visit?"

Edward looked to Bea and let her answer the reverend. "Twenty-four years."

"Twenty-four? That means this is the . . ."

"Yes, this is the year," she agreed.

"Goodness. No wonder everyone's talking about the candle."

The conversation ended soon after that. Nothing else seemed worthy of mentioning.

Reverend Richmond spent the night in the care of the soft-spoken churchwarden who had welcomed him at the parsonage. His Gladstone tour continued the next day. He met a farmer who showed him his flock. ("Purebred Cotswold sheep. My rams are famous.") And a retired tailor, inquisitive and cautious. ("Some of us were hoping for an older minister, you know.")

All in all, the villagers could not have been more friendly . . . or more untitled, rural, and backward. (One farmer asked Reverend Richmond if he'd ever delivered a lamb.) No match for an academician like himself.

He returned to Oxford the following day and awaited the next opportunity: the call from London, Southampton, or at least Bristol.

The don made it clear: no other options were coming. "Given the problems you've had, Gladstone is your only option."

"Gladstone doesn't fit me," he said, shrugging.

The Gladstonians held the same opinion. "Not quite right for us," was Barstow's tactful comment in his note to the Oxford don. The citizens returned to their routine, hoping for someone older, married—seasoned. A pastor with thick skin for the winters, a warm heart for farmers, and an open mind for the mystery of Christmas miracles and angel-touched candles.

He never came.

Reverend Richmond came.

He arrived in June. June labored into July. Summer cooled into autumn. Apple trees dropped fruit and then leaves. Maples turned a rusty tint, and blackthorn bushes produced their purple sloe berries. Early October felt the first freeze, and Gladstone's new minister purchased an extra blanket from Barstow's Mercantile.

As he made his selection, Emily Barstow watched. When he looked up, she blushed and looked away.

In the church vestment box, Reverend Richmond found a warmer cape to wear in the pulpit. It was this robe that he donned the first Advent Sunday in December, the day he refused to preach about the candle.

The young mother pulled the blanket over the face of her infant son. Even seated inside the train, she felt the chill of the December air.

"Ticket?"

She looked up to see the uniformed conductor.

"Oh yes." She'd forgotten to keep it handy. Reaching over her sleeping child, she found the ticket in her purse. The conductor checked it and handed it back.

"We'll warm up as the train leaves the station," encouraged the lady in the adjacent seat. She was matronly in appearance: gray hair peeking from beneath a bonnet, wrinkled face still red from the chill. "Long trip for you and the baby?"

"All day," Abigail said.

"I'll keep you company then." The lady looked around the crowded car. "Lots of travelers. Busy season."

The young mother nodded, cradled her son closer, and looked out the window at the sea of travelers. All wore coats and hats; most carried bags or children. Everyone was in a hurry to go somewhere. The train lurched, and Abigail grabbed the seat, then smiled at her neighbor.

"Jerky things, these trains," the woman sympathized.

Iron wheels slowly rolled the locomotive, mother, and child out of Paddington Station and into the city. Buildings passed, signs blurred, and Abigail felt moisture form in the corner of her eyes. She looked down at her sleeping son and spoke softly so no one would hear. "Are we doing the right thing, little man?" Then, as if answering for him, she asked, "What else can we do?"

She sighed, reached into her bag, and extracted a large brown envelope. She looked at the address, ran a thumb across her printed name, removed the letter, and did what she'd done a dozen times in the last twenty-four hours. She unfolded it and stared at the words. She thumbed away another tear.

"Are you all right?" asked the lady.

Abigail nodded but didn't look up. "This letter. I, uh, I can't read. But my landlord read it to me. So I was just looking at it."

"Would you like me to read it to you?"

Abigail smiled. "I would like that very much." She handed her neighbor the paper and looked down into the face of her child and listened as the woman read.

FIRST SUNDAY
OF ADVENT

December 4, 1864

As Edward took his seat in the church, he heard snatches of conversations, enough random sentences to reveal the topic on everyone's mind.

"If I get the candle, I know what I'll pray for . . ."

"I hear Edward already knows who he'll give it to . . ."

"Do you suppose he'd talk to me about it?"

Edward was relieved to see Bea take her seat at the hundred-year-old organ. Now the service would begin and the whisperings cease. People followed the cue of the ten-member choir as they stood to sing "Come, Thou Almighty King." Limestone walls echoed with "Praise God, from whom all blessings flow . . ." As the congregation sang, Edward looked out the window and spotted the reverend walking from the parsonage through the cemetery. As he leaned into the bracing wind, he held the neck of his coat closed and then loosened it as he neared the doors of the church.

I wonder what Reverend Richmond has prepared to say to us, Edward considered. He knew what Reverend Pillington would have said. He had understood the cherished place the candle held in the lives of Cotswold villagers. They endured difficult days: crawling out of bed on dark, cold mornings; closing the barn after the sun had set; sewing by the light of the fire; laboring through weeks of rainy, sunless seasons. The former rector had understood the life of the villagers and how the legend of the candle always lifted their spirits. Were he preaching today, he'd speak of surprises and angels and fresh hope in the midst of dark Decembers. He'd speak about the candle.

"No. I can't do that," the young minister had told Edward earlier in the week. "I'm not Pillington. I don't preach about candles. People don't need old wives' tales."

"But this is . . ."

"I know. This is the year. But I give people practical help and solid facts. I stay away from mysteries."

"You don't believe, do you?"

"I believe in the Bible. I believe in the church. I believe in God. But I see no reason to promote superstitions or raise false hopes."

"Don't you think God can work however he chooses?"

"I believe God worked, and the rest is up to us."

So, as the singing ceased and the choir took their seats, Edward shifted in his pew, anxious to hear what the reverend would say.

The congregation heard the click of Richmond's boots as he ascended the stone steps to the pulpit. He looked nervously over his flock and unfolded his notes with the ease of a suitor asking for a maid's hand in marriage.

He spoke of Christmas kindness and neighborly

love and Christian charity. Most other churches would have appreciated the message. But not the parishioners of St. Mark's. As they left the building, some refused to shake the reverend's hand. Others did so with disappointment. "The candle?" they asked. "Did you forget?"

Edward tried to hide his frustration but had trouble doing so. "Your sermon could have been better, Reverend." He then followed Bea as she and Sarah exited the nave.

"Nothing!" Sarah whispered. "He didn't say a word, not one word!"

"Perhaps it's for the best," Bea replied.

"People are already so . . ."

"Persistent," Edward finished for her.

"Persistent, indeed," Bea continued.

Chapter 4

MONDAY

December 12, 1864

An outside noise interrupted Edward's sleep. He opened his eyes and stared into the dark, not wanting to climb from beneath the covers. The bell in the ancient tower struck the five o'clock hour with lingering vibrations, as if its teeth were chattering in the belfry.

"It's cold," he muttered, as he snuggled up to his wife.

He was almost back to sleep when he heard the noise again. This time Bea heard it too.

"Edward," she whispered, "did you hear that?"

"Probably just a hedgehog."

"Go and see."

"It's freezing, Bea." But even as he protested, he knew he had to go. He grumbled and obliged.

He grabbed his coat off the back of the chair, threw it on over his nightshirt, and opened the door.

Moonlight illuminated a shivering hump against the wall of his house.

"Bea! Someone is out here!"

"Actually, Edward, there are two of us."

"James, Elizabeth, what are you doing?" Edward asked.

"Waiting on you," the woman answered, making ghosts with her breath.

By now Bea, wrapped in her bed's blanket, stood next to her husband. "Come in, you two," she urged. "You'll die of chill."

They were only too happy to oblige.

As the couple settled in by the fire, Edward begged for an explanation.

"Can we warm up a bit first?" James requested with trembling chin.

In short order Bea filled four cups with tea. The unsolicited guests wrapped their hands around the warmth and sighed as they sipped.

James and Elizabeth Clemly ran the Queen's Tavern south of town in a century-old building they rented from the lord of the manor in Chipping Campden. The two served as the first line of hospitality for Gladstone-bound travelers. As he offered hay and rest to the horses, she filled pints and plates in the pub. This morning they had walked the length of Bristol Road in the predawn darkness.

Edward's curiosity mounted as the couple's cups emptied. He was soon drumming the table with his fingers. "What is this all about?" he finally asked.

Elizabeth looked at James. He bore a heavy salt-and-pepper beard and a mop of matted hair. He pulled off his hat and wrung it like a wet rag and looked toward Elizabeth, who urged him on by pressing her lips together.

"The missus and I have a request."

A request? Edward was puzzled.

James squeezed his hat again and shifted forward in his chair. "Me and Elizabeth were wondering . . . You know I never ask anything of you, Edward. I always pay what I owe."

"That you do," the chandler offered. "So how can we help you?"

"My luck ran out. A couple of months back I was rollin' quite nice in a game in the pub. All cards were comin' my way. I knew I couldn't lose, so I bet it all. I even bet the next six months' earnings. Every shilling."

Elizabeth groaned.

James looked down at the floor and said, "I lost."

"You lost?"

"Everything. Elizabeth still has a few pence, but that's all we have left."

Edward scratched his head. "Well, I can't say that I know much about cards, but if you're looking for some advice, I know a fellow in Bibury—"

"The candle!" Elizabeth blurted.

"The candle?" Edward asked.

"Edward," offered Bea in a firm tone, "the Christmas Candle. After the angel's visit, they would like us to give them the candle."

"We're broke, Edward," James said. "The lord of the manor wants his rent money, and, well, he has been wanting it for two months now. He's talking eviction."

"Oh, I don't think . . . Surely he would listen to you."

"He won't. We've tried. Edward, you're our only hope."

"I see." Edward looked at Bea for a few moments, then at the floor and back to his friend.

"Well, you know, James, your need poses a bit of a problem." He cleared his throat. We're still a week from the angel's coming, and many people have already stopped by."

Bea kept her hand on Elizabeth's as Edward continued his explanation. The same explanation he had given the farmer whose oldest son had broken his leg just before harvest, leaving the farmer shorthanded. "I left a year's earnings in the field. I could use a miracle."

The same explanation he had given to Widow Leonard. Too old to work, she lived on what she took in from renting out the back of her house. She told Edward how new tenants were hard to find and how there wouldn't be enough money to buy coal for the rest of the winter.

"The Smith family needs help too," Edward continued. "They have twins, you know, sweetest little things. Have you seen them? Why, when Mrs. Smith walked in my shop with one in each arm—"

"Edward," Bea interrupted, once again bumping him back on track.

"Oh yes. Well, she fears for their health. And then Phineas Austen dropped by. Let's see, Bea, was it last Friday? Saturday? No matter. His wife is losing her sight. You've seen her. She's using a cane now. All those years of making . . . What is it she makes, dear?"

"Bonnets, Edward. She stitches lace on bonnets."

"She's going blind, and that's what I thought Phineas wanted to discuss. But he is more concerned about their son. He's in trouble with the law, and they fear"—by now Edward was lighting his pipe—"That he may"—he stopped midsentence to take a couple of puffs from his pipe—"End up in prison."

James stared at the floor, and Elizabeth leaned her forehead into her fingers.

"And who was it that came yesterday after Sunday services, Bea?"

"I believe you've made your point, Edward."

"I have?"

"Yes, you have," James assured. "Many requests. Many requests. I just thought . . . We just thought that, well . . ."

Bea slid her chair next to Elizabeth's. "We do understand. And we will pray. That's all we can do. Pray. We don't know why God has given us this gift. But we pray that he will direct us. He did before."

Elizabeth nodded. "I think often of Charles Barstow," she said. "Twenty-five years ago—before you gave him the candle—he was as directionless as a ship with no rudder. Now look at him. He is a fine man, fine indeed. You chose well."

"God led us then, and he will again. Now," Bea said, "we've all got work to do."

Bea and Edward stood in the doorway as their visitors departed. Edward wrapped an arm around his wife, and she asked, "What are we going to do? So many people need the candle. How can we decide who to give it to?"

Edward said nothing.

"I've been thinking," Bea said.

"About what?"

"That we could use the candle for ourselves. Our need is as deep as they come."

Edward shook his head slowly. "I don't know, dear. Our family has always given it away."

"But has any Haddington faced what we're facing?"

Edward reached across and took her hand. "We'll see. We'll see."

Abigail passed the morning the way she had begun it: seated on a train, holding her baby, pondering the words of the letter. London streets gave way to England countryside. Even under the blanket of winter, the hills maintained their charm. Abigail could see villages in each valley marked by tall towers, gabled roofs, and clustering elms.

It felt good to be going home. She just wished for different circumstances. Her fingers twisted the corner of her baby's blanket as if her hands needed something to hold on to. Will it be the same? *She wondered.*

SATURDAY
EVENING

December 17, 1864

Guests occupied every corner of the Barstow parlor. With full bellies and filled glasses, they lingered long after the meal. Charles Barstow discussed politics with two guests from Upper Slaughter. Mr. Chumley listened politely to an elderly friend's complaints about arthritis. Mrs. Barstow relayed the latest gossip on romance and marriage.

Bea and Edward had declined the invitation to dinner. Everyone understood why. This was, after all, the night. The eve of the final Advent Sunday. They had preparations to make, a guest to receive.

The reverend, however, had accepted the Barstows' invitation.

"You came." Emily brightened as he arrived. In six months the two had shared no more than six sentences, but he had noticed her watching him.

"I saw you last week joking with the Johnson children," she noted as the two talked.

The rector smiled, pleased to be caught in an act of kindness. "I, uh, I enjoy them. Their mother is sick, you know."

"I know."

"The twelve-year-old asks me many questions."

"Does he?"

"Great questions. Questions of faith and God."

"Like?"

The reverend's voice animated just slightly. "The other day he mused, 'How do we know we aren't butterflies dreaming we are humans?'"

Emily smiled. "And you told him?"

"I told him, 'That's a good question.'"

The two laughed, and his face softened.

"You should do that more often," Emily urged.

"Do what?"

"Laugh!" She clapped her hands. "I never see you laugh."

Richmond looked down at his tea.

"Do you find Gladstone dull?" she ventured.

"Dull? Of course not . . ."

Her eyes betrayed her disbelief, so he adjusted his response, admitting, "At first, yes. I confess, my heart was set on going elsewhere."

"London?"

"I was raised there. My father is a friend of the bishop. It made sense that I serve in London."

"But . . ."

"London was not an option."

"I thought you had family connections."

"Other factors were considered." As soon as the words left his mouth, the reverend's face flushed, and he looked away. Emily waited for him to continue, but he didn't.

"The candle." Emily finally changed the subject. "You must know everyone is upset that you aren't saying anything about the candle in your sermons."

"Yes, I know."

"I don't understand. Don't you believe in it?"

"I can't encourage false hope. I want no part of disappointing people."

"And the candle disappoints people?"

"How can it not? One candle. A village of needs. God would not single out one person and ignore the others. It's not fair."

Emily replied with measured words. "Perhaps he singles out one person to show the others what he can do."

The reverend started to speak, then stopped. "Can I think about that?"

She smiled her yes.

"Excuse me, but Sarah and I are bidding our farewells," Mr. Chumley interrupted.

"Our bedtime nears. We aren't young like you," Sarah added. "Have you had a good evening?"

"Quite." The minister nodded.

"Tomorrow's a working day for you, Reverend. Are you ready with a sermon?"

"Indeed it is, and that I am."

With a wry smile Mr. Chumley looked at the young minister. "And all this talk about the candle. Are you converted yet, or do you still stand with me on the cynic's side of the fence?"

"Mr. Chumley," Sarah interrupted her husband, "the hour is too late to wade into another discussion. Let's get your hat and cane."

"I suppose we'll know more soon. Good night."

"I suppose we shall," Reverend Richmond agreed. "Good night to you both."

The young couple watched the Chumleys leave.

After some time Richmond spoke. "I suppose I should leave as well."

"Perhaps we could visit again?" Emily risked.

He started to speak, stopped, then continued. "I'm not who you think I am, Emily. I'm not as hard as the village thinks, nor am I as good as you think. I've made mistakes and . . ."

"And mistakes are to be put in the past."

"Emily?" Mr. Barstow called from the door. "Can you join us? Our guests are leaving."

"Certainly, Grandfather," she answered but turned to the minister first and with a slight smile repeated, "in the past."

Chapter 6

LATE SATURDAY NIGHT

December 17, 1864

A dancing fire warmed Edward's shop, and two hanging lanterns illuminated it. Bea kept him company, rocking and knitting in the corner.

He enjoyed talking as he worked, and Bea didn't mind listening.

"Did I tell you about the merchant from Ironbridge I

61

met at the pub?" He measured twine as he talked, cutting it into ten-inch strips.

"I don't think you did."

"He told me about Thomas Trevor, a chandler who works near the coal mines. He employs four workers twelve hours a day. With the five of them, they produce nearly five thousand candles a week."

"I can't imagine the sort."

"Why, the most I can ever sell in Gladstone is a hundred a week. Although here I am preparing thirty for tomorrow alone."

"Tomorrow's different."

Edward completed his cutting and began wrapping the twine on one of the three rods of his dipping rack.

"This Trevor fellow has a tool he calls the 'nodding donkey.' It rotates like an indoor windmill, holding six racks, with each holding thirty or so candles by the wicks as they dry. He even has a machine for cutting the wicks. He sets a dozen spools in a tray, stretches the strings across a table, and lowers the blade on them. He calls it a guillotine."

"I can see why."

"You haven't heard the half of it. Trevor makes some of the candles green."

Bea lowered her needles and looked up. "Who wants green candles?"

"Mine owners do. It seems that some of their workers find the tallow tasty and have taken to chewing it. Others think the wax protects their throats from the dust. For whatever reason, miners chew the candles, eating up the mine owner's property and profits."

"But green candles?"

"The color sticks to the mouth. When a foreman spots a worker with green lips and tongue, he boots him out."

Bea shook her head and placed her knitting in a basket. "It's not worth a candle."

"Indeed not."

"I'm going to the house, but I'll be back."

"Bundle up."

Edward tied the last of the strips of twine to the rack, took it by either side, and walked across the shop. He lowered the thirty strings into the tub of hot tallow long enough for the waxy substance to cling and then lifted them out. As he repeated the process again and again, the candles began to thicken, and his thoughts began to wander.

Blame it on the late hour or significant night or both,

but Edward grew nostalgic, reflective. "How many times have I done this? How many hours in this shop?" he asked aloud to no one but himself. "My, it's been good. Good wife, friends . . . faith."

Cold air rushed into the room. He turned and saw Bea standing in the doorway. The fireplace glow silhouetted her frame. Her face was left in shadows, and for a moment he saw her as she had looked at age twenty-five. Slim figure. Her hair burnt orange, as bright as a summer sunset, reminding him of the night fifty years earlier when they had first seen the angel.

Edward's reverie was interrupted by the sound of his wife's voice. "Edward? Did you hear me? Would you like some tea?"

"Yes. That would be nice." Edward, content with the width of the candles, suspended the rack on eye-level ceiling hooks in the center of the shop.

Bea handed him a cup, and the two stood looking at the rack.

"Remember fifty years ago?" he asked. "The first candle we gave?"

"To Reverend Pillington. How could I forget?"

"He and I were the same age."

"He was a year younger perhaps. But he was so desperate to believe."

Edward nodded. "I remember feeling odd giving a candle of faith to a man of faith."

"Purveyors of hope need it the most."

"God blessed him. And blessed Gladstone through him." Edward lowered his tea. "May he rest in peace."

The candlemaker cleaned the tallow tub and stoked the fire. Only then did he notice that Bea had left the shop again. She returned with a bottle and held it up as she closed the door. "Apple wine?"

"A gift from Elizabeth?"

"Nice to be bribed."

She filled two cups and handed one to him. He lifted his as a toast. "To the last candle."

"To the last candle."

They again took their seats by the fire, and for a time neither spoke.

"The house is quiet this year," said Bea.

"Painfully so."

Bea turned toward her husband. "Can we talk about the candle again? Do we have to give it away? Would it be so bad if we kept it for ourselves?"

"Now, Bea. I don't know if it is intended for us."

"Maybe, since it's the last one, this candle is a gift to the Haddington family. Maybe?"

"Perhaps. The Lord knows we could use a miracle." He lit his pipe, and the two rocked in silence.

"Staying awake?" she finally asked.

"Why certainly," he pledged.

Good intentions, however, gave way to weary bodies. Little by little their eyelids drooped and heads lowered. Before the fire had embered, their heads rested, chins on chests, and the candlemaker and his wife were sound asleep.

The light woke them. Brilliant, explosive, and shocking light. December midnight became July noonday. Edward needed a moment to come to his senses. He couldn't remember why he was sleeping in a chair and not in his bed. As Edward rubbed his eyes with the heels of his hands, Bea nudged him.

Her whisper had force. "Edward! The angel!"

He looked straight into the light, squinting as if looking into the sun. He distinguished a silhouette.

The angel lifted an illuminated hand and paused as if to make certain the couple was watching. He took a step in the direction of the rack. Edward and Bea leaned forward. The angel touched a candle toward the end of the third row—and then disappeared. The candle glowed for a few seconds against the now-darkened room.

As the light diminished, Bea urged, "Edward! The candle!"

If only he had kept his eyes on it. If only he hadn't looked away to see where the angel went. If only his foot hadn't gone to sleep. Then the calamity might have been averted, but it wasn't.

Edward took a step on his tingling foot and lost his balance. As he fell face forward, he thrust one hand high in the air, hoping to grab the just-touched candle. Instead, he hit the rack and knocked it off the hooks, sending thirty candles—thirty identical candles—flying around the room.

Edward looked up at Bea. Bea looked down at Edward. Horrified. They sprang to their feet and raced around the shop, examining candles in the hope that one of them might contain a glimmer of light. None did.

After a few moments both plopped into their chairs, hands full of candles. Neither had the slightest notion which candle had been touched by the angel.

Bea burst into tears. "Now what? We have thirty candles. One of them is special, and we don't know which!" She buried her face in her hands. Edward stared at the floor.

As the shock wore off, Bea spoke up. "You'll have to make a new batch for tomorrow's Advent service. We can't risk giving away the angel candle."

"I will. We'll save this batch until we know what to do."

Bea set the thirty candles in a basket, and Edward got busy in the shop.

Chapter 7

SUNDAY

December 18, 1864

After church the next morning, Edward and Bea were the center of attention.

"Visitors last night?"

"Any candles to distribute this week?" Wink.

"Come see me tomorrow, Bea. I'll make biscuits." Wink. Wink.

Later that afternoon Edward decided to go for a

walk. "I need to get outside for a while, dear. Would you like to come?"

Bea declined. "You go ahead."

But as he left the house, she stopped him. "Take these." Bea handed him the basket of candles from the night before.

"Why?"

"I don't know. God may tell you what to do with them."

Edward stopped by the livery stable to greet his old friend Adam Patterson. Adam was tall and lean and ever happy and could make Edward feel as if the day revolved around his arrival. This day, however, there was no cheerful shout from within the stables, no slap on the back or offer of tea and biscuits. Edward found Adam in a horse stall, seated on a stool, leaning against a wall.

"Adam?" Edward hurried to his side.

"What is wrong?"

His friend didn't look up. "It's my head, Edward. It pounds and pounds."

"When did this start?"

"Last week."

"Why didn't you tell me?"

"You've been busy with the candle."

"Have you talked to Mr. Chumley?"

"I have. He has no solution." Adam looked up for the first time. "My father, Edward. Remember?"

Edward remembered. Years before, Adam's father had complained of the same symptoms and had died within a week.

Still looking at Edward, Adam said, "My friend, I know I ask much. But God must have guided you to me for a reason. Tell me. Do you still have the candle?"

The candlemaker pulled a stool next to Adam and sat. "I do," he answered. He had the candle; he just didn't know where. Yet how could he admit this to Adam? The pain had paled his friend's face and left his hands trembling. Edward sighed and made his decision. He reached into his basket and handed Adam a candle. "Take this, my friend. God will hear your prayers."

Adam's eyes misted with gratitude. Edward's heart clouded with confusion. What had he done? How dare he give hope? But how dare he not? Adam was his friend, and, who knows, he *might* have given his friend the Christmas Candle.

Edward requested, "Let's keep this our secret."

"Whatever you say."

After some time the candlemaker left the livery stable and continued his walk. James Clemly spotted him on the street. When the pub owner requested a moment to chat, Edward guessed the topic. "The lord of the manor needs his rent, and I need some help."

Edward motioned for James to follow, and the men stepped between two buildings. Having already given a candle at the livery stable, it seemed easier to do so again. James embraced him. Again Edward suggested secrecy. "Perhaps it's best that you not tell anyone."

"Sure," agreed the bright-eyed James. "The element of surprise, right?"

How will I explain this to Bea? Edward wondered.

He returned to the house and said little. He wanted to tell her what he had done but couldn't find the words.

"I'll be in the shop." He placed the candle basket on the table and walked out the door.

When Sarah dropped in for afternoon tea, Bea told her sister about the visitors and hint droppers. Sarah grew quiet. "Bea," she said, stirring her drink, "if I had any other options, I wouldn't trouble you. But I have none."

Bea extended her hand across the table and covered her sister's. "Sarah, what is it?"

"I married a dear man, Bea. He cares as much for me today as the day we married. But even after all these years and all our prayers, he still has no faith. His world consists of what he sees and touches." She paused to dab a tear. "We're living our autumn years, dear sister."

Bea nodded. "We're both living with unanswered prayers, are we not?"

Sarah squeezed Bea's hand. "What am I doing, sharing concerns with you? You have enough troubles of your own."

"Sarah," Bea spoke firmly, "don't worry about us. Something is on your mind. What is it?"

"I'm thinking of the candle, dear sister. Is there any way . . ."

Bea sighed. "Let me tell you what happened Saturday night." She described the light and the touch of the angel. When she told about Edward's stumble, the two sisters laughed until they cried. And as they filled the house with happiness, Bea made a decision.

She stopped short of telling her sister the whole story. She didn't mention that they didn't know which candle the angel had blessed. Bea reached into the basket. "Here, Sarah. For you. For your husband's faith."

Sarah clutched the gift to her chest and beamed, her face awash with tears.

"Perhaps it's best to tell no one for now," Bea said.

"Of course."

The two stood and embraced. As she watched her sister leave, Bea asked herself, *How will I explain this to Edward?*

She was asking herself the same question an hour later as Emily Barstow walked quickly away from the shop, a candle tucked under her shawl. *She only wants the young reverend to notice her. How could I not give her hope?*

Standing at the doorway to their home that evening, Edward and Bea could see the villagers walking toward the church.

"Should we go join them?" Bea asked.

"Let's stay home. I need to tell you what I did today."
He told it all. Adam's headaches, James's request. "I gave candles to them both. Have I done a horrible thing?"

Bea said nothing. Edward thought she was angry. "What have I done?" he asked.

"Exactly what I did," she confessed and then shared the details of Sarah and Emily. "People will be so angry, so hurt. All our friends will think we deceived them."

"But we didn't mean to mislead anyone, dear."

"I know, but we did. What will they think when their prayers go unanswered? We should have kept all the candles."

"And leave the special candle in the basket?"

"We can't do that, either."

"Bea, we did the only thing we could. We gave candles, hoping to give the right one."

"So what do we do now? Give them all?"

Edward sighed. "Do we have a choice? How else can we be sure that someone will receive the Christmas Candle?"

"True." She nodded, then smiled. "Edward, now we can light a candle too."

"I suppose we can," he said.

❦

Abigail knew little about Oxford, but she didn't need to know much. The walk from the train station to the carriage house was brief and direct. The gray cloud cover and fog muffled the noonday sun. She was tempted to find a room and rest. But she knew better. Wait too long and she might lose her courage.

She made her way through the winding streets and boarded the covered cart. Left to her own means, she could never afford the passage in a carriage.

But the courier who had delivered the letter had delivered money as well.

Other passengers dozed as the wagon bounced. She couldn't. Her mind kept returning to the words of the letter . . . By now she knew them almost by heart.

MONDAY

December 19, 1864

Early the next morning Reverend Richmond knocked on the Haddingtons' door. Bea answered it. "Merry Christmas, Reverend. Won't you come in?"

"Edward, I need to speak with you about this candle business," he began. His tone was less than cordial. "People expect me to mention it in the Christmas Eve service."

"Yes, they do."

"To ask the recipient of the candle to stand."

"That's the tradition."

"How can I? This is superstition. Have you seen the parishioners? They are counting on the candle to help them . . . to save them . . . to rescue them . . ."

"It's not the candle that can save them, Reverend. It's the Giver of it."

"This is disastrous."

Edward and Bea had never seen him so worked up.

"You should preach like this," Edward offered.

"Edward," Bea buffered.

"What do you mean?" The reverend frowned.

"With passion. Your preaching could use some. A little pulpit fire never burned a church, you know. Why, Reverend Pillington . . ."

"I weary of hearing about Reverend Pillington."

The trio sat in embarrassed silence for a few moments. Edward finally spoke up. "What are you afraid of, Reverend? Afraid the prayers won't be answered or afraid they will?"

The young rector started to speak, then stopped.

Edward continued in soft yet firm tones. "The

mystery of God unsettles us all, Reverend. But isn't mystery where God works? If he does only what we understand, is he God?"

He paused, inviting the rector to reply. He didn't. Nor did he look away. Edward opted for bluntness. "Do you fear that God will dash the faith of the people, my son? Or do you fear that he will stretch yours?"

Reverend Richmond's face softened for a moment. Then it hardened. "All this talk of angels and hope. Where will it lead us?"

"And your dismissal of miracles . . . Where will that lead us?"

The reverend started to object, but Bea placed a motherly hand on his and, for the first time, addressed him by his Christian name. "David, something burdens you. What is it?"

The young minister said nothing.

Edward leaned forward. "The first day we met I asked you why Gladstone. You seem groomed for the cathedral, a city like Gloucester, not a country parish. You never answered that question. Perhaps this would be a good time to do so."

Reverend Richmond pressed his two hands into a

tent and leaned his lips into them. After several moments he lifted his eyes and began to speak.

"Four of us were at a pub. It was a year ago . . . a year this month. We were celebrating the coming holidays. The winter night was cold, the ale was good, and the fire was warm. So we drank. We drank until we, well, we became foolish, foolish and loud.

"Patrons told us to be quiet. The pub owner threatened to throw us out. I told him my father's name and position and dared him to do so. He didn't hesitate.

"Next thing I knew we were standing outside, bracing against the cold. The wind was bitter and I was too. The man had humiliated me in front of my friends. Embarrassment prompted me to do something I'll regret for the rest of my life.

"I saw an empty delivery wagon in the street, still hitched to its team. I jumped on, grabbed the reins, and told my friends to go with me. They hesitated . . . so I prodded. 'What are you, afraid?' They finally climbed up.

"I was imagining a fast ride, a few laughs. We'd have the wagon back at the pub before anyone missed it."

The reverend looked down.

"What happened?" Edward asked.

"Something horrible. I had no business handling a wagon. The wind was strong, I was drunk and inexperienced. I slapped the reins and off we went. I feigned being in control. My buddies knew better. They told me to slow down, go back. But no, I had my pride.

"A narrow bridge crosses the Thames a mile north of the pub. The road bends sharply just before the crossing. The turn demands care on a clear day with a good driver. A drunk one on a dark, icy night has no hope. I missed it entirely. When I knew what was happening, I pulled up, but it was too late. The horses, the wagon, we all plunged over the edge of a steep ravine and fell fifteen feet into the water.

"All of a sudden I was fighting to stay afloat. Three of us made it to the river's edge. We looked frantically for George, our friend. We stomped up and down the bank, crying out his name, crying out to God.

"We had to abandon the search—we were freezing. We found a house and got help. They located his body the next morning."

The trio sat in silence for a long time.

Bea was the first to speak. "I'm so sorry, son. You must be heartbroken."

"More than you could imagine. I was so stupid, so

childish. I got what I deserved. But my friend . . . he didn't deserve to die. I suppose that's why I see God in the fashion I do."

He turned and looked straight at Bea, lower lip quivering. "God could have helped. He should have helped. I used to think he hears us when we pray. But I prayed that night. With all my heart . . . Now, I don't know anymore."

"This is how you ended up in Gladstone?" Edward asked.

Richmond nodded. "We should have been expelled. My father intervened, however. But the don made it clear I would never know the likes of a preferred pulpit. I guess Gladstone is my penance."

"Or," Edward adjusted, "Gladstone is where you find forgiveness."

Bea looked at her husband. "It's all right that we tell him, don't you think?"

"About Abigail?" he answered.

The clergyman looked at her. "Tell me what?"

"We didn't tell you the whole story. The fact is, our granddaughter used to live with us . . . until a year ago. She ran away last January. We think she is in London; a friend saw her there last spring."

"Why did she leave?"

"She made a mistake she must have thought we couldn't forgive," Bea explained.

"We've tried to find her," Edward added. "Believe me, we've tried."

Bea walked across the room and lifted a candle from the basket. "I guess we all need Christmas miracles, don't we, David?"

She handed the candle to the minister. "Take this, my son. You need some light."

He smiled. "I don't think I should . . ."

"Just take it."

He placed the candle in his coat and stood to leave. As Edward opened the door, he made a request. "Follow the tradition in the Christmas Eve service. Who knows what might happen?"

Edward and Bea watched him walk away, then Edward closed the door.

"Bea," Edward invited, "we have one more candle."

She knew his thoughts and smiled. He set the candle in the holder; the two sat at the table and prayed. They prayed for forgiveness, faith, and a young girl in a large city.

Chapter 9

CHRISTMAS EVE

December 24, 1864

The candle basket was now empty. Thirty hopeful Gladstonians guarded their candles and secrets and looked for a miracle. A ten-year-old girl prayed for her arguing parents. The family of a sailor prayed for his safe arrival. A wife prayed for her husband to sober up. Reverend Richmond had never seen so many weekday visitors stopping to pray.

As the Christmas Eve service drew nigh, however, Edward and Bea expressed occasional bouts with doubt. "What will people do to us when they realize we gave them common candles?" Bea asked.

"Do you think your uncle in Preston could give us a place to live?" Edward teased, only partly in jest.

"Credibility. Friends. Candle shop. We could lose it all," Bea listed.

"Still, we have to attend the service, if for no other reason than to explain."

"They won't believe us," Bea lamented.

Edward planned his words and mentally rehearsed them over and over. By Saturday night he was ready. They waited until the singing had begun before stepping out into the cold night and walking to the church for the Christmas Eve service. The streets were empty; everyone was in St. Mark's.

"Well, dear husband, only God knows what awaits us."

"At least one person will be happy to see us."

The couple found space on the back pew and took a seat. Strands of garland draped between the windows, and a row of flames flickered in each sill. The children's nativity play was in full swing. Emily Barstow had organized the cast and props. The locksmith played one of the wise men, as did Adam from the livery stable. A homemade doll rested in the manger, and a lamb kept bumping it over with her nose. Laughter and applause bounced off the church's stone walls.

Reverend Richmond began his welcome. "We thank the ladies who cleaned the floors, our men who repaired the door. We appreciate the Haddingtons for the window candles."

Several heads swiveled and looked at the couple. Edward and Bea kept their eyes on Reverend Richmond.

"This is my first Christmas Eve service with you," the reverend continued. "I understand that the church traditionally begins this gathering with testimonies and announcements of blessings. We have all been blessed, far more than we deserve. Yet I am told that among us sits one person who has benefited from an angel's touch." He paused, looked over the audience, and invited, "Could I ask that soul to stand?"

Edward and Bea gulped. She closed her eyes. He took her hand and whispered, "We'll be all right, dear." He bowed his head and offered a silent prayer. Lord, these are your people, your flock. Look with kindness upon this moment.

He heard the congregation begin to murmur. "What is this?" someone asked aloud. Another wondered, "How can this be?" Then a third, "What is going on?" Edward assumed the worst. *No one is standing.*

But when he and Bea opened their eyes, they couldn't believe what they saw: people standing all over the sanctuary.

Reverend Richmond took a step back from the pulpit. "I don't understand. Why so many of you?"

Villagers began asking for permission to say a word. The reverend called on a farmer on the front row. "You know me, Edward." He turned and spoke across the crowd. "I can't resist the bottle. But since you gave me the candle, I've been here, in prayer, each evening. Why others are standing, I can't say, but I haven't touched a drop in four days."

"Reverend," requested another man, "may I?" The young minister nodded, and James stood. "My landlord and I have been at odds for months about the rent. But last Sunday, Edward gave me the candle. The missus and I prayed, and yesterday the landlord came to me and said, 'Who am I to make demands? Apart from God's mercy, I would have nothing,' and then he gave me a clean slate and said he'd extend more credit if I needed it."

Adam, from the livery, spoke next. "Like you, Reverend, I'm bewildered by this response. I know this, however: my head is better. Not healed, but better."

The Widow Leonard rose. "I rented out the back of my house."

A man stood up next to her. "And I found a place to live."

Even Emily raised her hand. Looking directly at the minister, she said, "I'm not sure he notices me, but the more I pray, the more I know God does."

Blessing after blessing.

"My husband's been gone since summer. But he promises he's back to stay."

"Our son is back from sea."

"Mr. Barstow hired me at the mercantile. I don't have to sell my farm."

Edward and Bea watched with wide eyes and listened with happy hearts. Finally, after a harvest of good news, Edward stood. "I need to say something."

He walked down the aisle, turned, and looked into the weathered faces of the villagers.

Digging his hands deep in his pockets, he began, "The night the angel came something happened that no one expected."

He told them the story, every detail: the deep slumber, the glowing light, the tingling foot, and the fall. (All chuckled at this point.) "Who has the real Christmas Candle? Only God knows, but he does know. And I know he uses the mistakes of stumblers." He cast a knowing glance at the reverend. "And he has heard our prayers.

"Perhaps we trusted the candle too much. Perhaps we trusted God too little. So God took our eyes off the candle and set them on himself. He is the Candle of Christmas. And Gladstone? Gladstone is one of his Bethlehems. For he has come to us all."

A chorus of *amens* boomed in the church.

"Bea, I've preached enough. Come to the organ. It's time to sing!"

Bea played every Christmas carol she knew, from "God Rest Ye Merry, Gentlemen" to "Hark! The Herald Angels Sing." Queen Victoria heard no sweeter music than St. Mark's did that Christmas Eve.

But midway through "Silent Night" the service came to a frightening halt. The entrance doors slammed open, and a disheveled man ran in screaming, "Help! Someone help!" Sudden air gusted, whipping the flames on back window candles. Singing stopped and a hundred heads turned toward the rear of the sanctuary.

Edward, with a clear view from his aisle seat, recognized the man as the driver of the coach wagon. He was a stark contrast to the worshippers—they, gleeful and warm; he, saucer-eyed and freezing. Ice clung to his beard and fear hung from his words. Grasping for breath, he sputtered, "One side of the bridge . . . Collins Bridge . . . it gave way."

Gladstonians gasped at the thought. "Are you hurt?" someone shouted.

"No . . . my passengers . . . they fell over the side. I looked for them, but it's too dark."

"Them?" Richmond asked. He stepped up the aisle toward the man. "Who was with you?"

"A girl and her baby. The other passengers got off at Upper Slaughter. We should have stayed the night there, it's so cold and icy. But she insisted."

Richmond spun toward the front of the church.

"Hurry. The creek is shallow. She may be all right. All able-bodied men come with me."

"I'll have a fire going in my house," Sarah volunteered.

"I have extra lanterns in my pub," shouted James.

"And I have more in my store," Barstow offered.

"Get them. Grab blankets and rope as well," Richmond instructed. "We don't have a minute to waste. Adam, bring a wagon. This girl will be in no condition to walk."

"Certainly."

"Meet at the bridge! May God have mercy."

The moment the people said "amen," the midnight bells began to ring. Worshippers scurried into the frigid night under the commission of twelve chimes.

Chapter 10

MIDNIGHT

December 24, 1864

Clouds blocked stars and wind howled through the trees. Edward wrapped a scarf around his face and felt a stab of dread in his heart. *Could anyone survive this cold?* he wondered to himself.

He and Richmond were the first to leave St. Mark's. The reverend grabbed a lit lantern that hung by the exit, and Edward followed. They hurried down Bristol Lane onto the muddy, wagon-wheel rutted road. Edward stayed a step behind his young companion, benefiting from the light and the windbreak. Neither spoke for the ten minutes it took to reach Collins Bridge.

They paused for a moment at the crossing. One of the corner beams, weakened from weather and wear, tilted forward causing the bridge to slope steeply toward the water. The wagon remained on the suspension, thanks to the two horses standing firmly on dry ground. Edward envisioned the young mother, struggling to hold on, and then falling over the edge.

"Hurry, Edward, let's search downstream."

A gust of wind picked up as the two walked toward the ravine. Edward heard voices behind him and turned to see another set of lanterns. He couldn't distinguish the carriers and didn't wait to try.

"We're going on the west side," he yelled. "You cross over!"

"We will!" It was Mr. Chumley.

Edward caught up with Richmond, who was illuminating the slope with the lantern. "Be careful, Edward, it's muddy."

Edward tried his best but lost his footing and slid the five feet down the edge.

"I'm okay," he assured. "Just glad I wasn't holding the lantern."

"Indeed," Richmond agreed as the two began to slush their way along the bank.

"Any idea who the girl is?" Richmond yelled over the wind.

"No."

"Hello!" they cried. "Hello!" But they heard nothing.

The two were in the water as much as out of it. The steep slope and trees left them the slenderest path. The water soon soaked their boots, numbing their legs from the knees down. Richmond, with the lantern, led the way, careful not to advance too far ahead of Edward. He paused often to yell:

"Still there?"

"Yes, yes," Edward assured.

As it turned out, it was Richmond who took the fall. He ventured around a tree by stepping into the water, one hand on the trunk, the other holding the lantern. His foot slipped, and he and the lantern fell into the stream.

Edward saw the reverend splash and stopped in the abrupt darkness.

"I'm fine, Edward. I'm fine," he heard the reverend

assure. Through the inky night Edward made out the form of Richmond struggling to his feet and back to the shore.

"We have no light," the reverend bemoaned.

They heard the water rushing, leaves rustling, and then . . . from downstream, a call for help.

"Edward! Did you hear that?"

"I did."

The call came again. This time Edward responded. "We're coming!"

"But I can't see one step ahead of me!"

"Feel your way forward."

Richmond didn't budge. "I can't move. This is too familiar. The cold. The darkness. The water. Oh, God," he pleaded, "not again."

Edward placed a hand on his shoulder. "Don't give up on God, son."

Richmond folded his arms and shivered. As he did he felt something in his coat. A candle. The candle Edward had given him earlier.

"Do you have a match, Edward?"

"A match?"

"I found a candle in my pocket."

"It will do no good," he told Richmond. "The flame can't withstand the wind."

"It may for a moment. And a moment of light is better than none!"

Edward reached for the matches he kept to light his pipe. "Let's lean together and block the wind!"

The two stood side by side as Edward struck the match. It flared, then disappeared.

"Closer! Stand closer to me!" the candlemaker instructed.

Both men bent at the waist. Richmond held the candle as still as his shaking hands allowed. The match flame touched the wick, then expired.

"It's wet," Edward explained.

"One more time," Richmond urged.

Edward took another match, struck it, and held it toward the candle. Richmond cupped his hand around the wick. The flame held, dancing for a moment. "I think it's going to light."

It did more, much more. Before the two men could straighten, radiance exploded. The light of a dozen torches pushed back the darkness. A bonfire couldn't have been brighter. Edward could see the wide eyes and dropped jaw of the reverend. "What is happening?" Richmond asked.

"A miracle is happening, son. Hurry, these lights tend to pass quickly."

Richmond reached the girl first. She was on the ground, huddled against a tree, clutching a bundle to her breast. "Looks like she was trying to find her way out," Richmond suggested. He squatted and placed a hand on the girl's shoulder. "Are you all right?"

No response.

"Is she alive?" Edward asked.

Richmond removed his glove, lifted her chin, and placed two fingers beneath her scarf.

He scarcely breathed as he felt for a pulse. He never got one but didn't need one. The girl groaned.

"She's alive, Edward."

Richmond turned his attention to the child. He lifted the blanket and placed a hand beneath the small nose. "This one is fine too. Sound asleep, likely better off than the mother."

Noises emerged from behind them.

"What is this light?" Barstow asked as he and four others hurried to help.

"An answered prayer, Charles." Edward smiled. "Let's get these two out of the cold."

⚜

Richmond rode in the back of the wagon with Mr. Chumley, the mother, and the child. They covered the two with blankets. Edward sat in front with Adam. The rest of the men hurried along behind.

True to her word, Sarah had a blazing fire with which to welcome them. "She's drifting in and out of consciousness," Chumley told her. "Must have hit her head."

"Let me have the baby."

Chumley handed his wife the child, and he and Richmond carried the mother into the small parlor and seated her near the fire. Edward and Adam quickly followed. Within moments, all of Gladstone, it seemed, was in the room or on the porch.

Bea placed a warmed blanket on the girl's shoulders. "We'll let you rest a bit, then get you out of those wet clothes." As of yet, no one had seen the young mother's face. It was completely scarf-wrapped, leaving room only for a set of eyes that, Edward noticed, seemed to grow wider by the moment.

"There, there," motherly Bea comforted, offering a cup of tea. "This will help. Let me take your wrap."

Bea undraped the scarf as one unwraps a gift, and what Bea saw was the finest gift she could have imagined.

"Abigail!"

Edward leaned forward from the fire.

Sarah gasped.

Mr. Chumley shook his head. "It's Abigail."

"Abigail?" Richmond asked everyone.

"My granddaughter," Edward explained, as he knelt by the chair and embraced his prodigal child. Bea joined him, and, for the first time in too long, the three held each other and wept.

Abigail finally pushed back. "Papa, Grandmother . . . where is my baby?"

Sara handed her the child. Abigail slipped the blanket away from the baby's face. "I named him Edward."

Whispers of the news and name rippled across the room and out the door to the men on the porch.

Edward looked up and searched out the eyes of Reverend Richmond. "Looks like God still gives babies at Christmas," he winked.

"And light," the minister agreed. "He still gives light when we need it the most."

AND LATER . . .

I know it's dark. I should be home within an hour," the store owner assured his wife over the phone. He stared out the window at the snow-covered cars. "But tomorrow is Sunday, and I want to take the day off. Put the baby to bed. I'll be home soon, and we'll finish decorating the tree. Besides, I only have four more boxes to empty."

"Okay, dear. I'll take care."

He hung up and returned to the task. He cut open the cardboard and placed the candles side by side on the shelf. Each box contained different shapes, and each shape went to a different section of the store. By the time he finished, the shelves were full, and the time was well past the hour he had promised to be home.

Rather than hurry out, however, he sat at the desk to pay a few bills. "I'll feel better getting these ready," he justified. But he made it only halfway through the stack when he leaned over the desk and fell sound asleep on his arm.

The next thing he knew, light exploded in the room. He sat up and rubbed his eyes. Ed Haddington gulped as the figure within the flame extended a finger toward one of the fat candles on the lower shelf . . .

*I*t was an ordinary night with ordinary
sheep and ordinary shepherds . . .

Then the black sky exploded with brightness. Trees
that had been shadows jumped into clarity. Sheep
that had been silent became a chorus of curiosity. One
minute the shepherd was dead asleep, the next he was
rubbing his eyes and staring into the face of an alien.

The night was ordinary no more.

The angel came in the night because that is when lights
are best seen and that is when they are most needed.

THE APPLAUSE OF HEAVEN

Maybe He Is the Messiah

*O*nce there was a man whose life was one of misery. The days were cloudy, and the nights were long. Henry didn't want to be unhappy, but he was. With the passing of the years, his life had changed. His children were grown. The neighborhood was different. The city seemed harsher.

He was unhappy. He decided to ask his minister what was wrong.

"Am I unhappy for some sin I have committed?"

"Yes," the wise pastor replied. "You have sinned."

"And what might that sin be?"

"Ignorance," came the reply. "The sin of ignorance.

One of your neighbors is the Messiah in disguise, and you have not seen him."

The old man left the office stunned. "The Messiah is one of my neighbors?" He began to think whom it might be.

Tom the butcher? No, he's too lazy. Mary, my cousin down the street? No, too much pride. Aaron the paperboy? No, too indulgent. The man was confounded. Every person he knew had defects. But one was the Messiah. He began to look for him.

He began to notice things he hadn't seen. The grocer often carried the sacks to the cars of older ladies. *Maybe he is the Messiah.* The officer at the corner always had a smile for the kids. *Could it be?* And the young couple who'd moved next door. *How kind they are to their cat. Maybe one of them . . .*

With time he saw things in people he'd never seen. And with time his outlook on life began to change. The bounce returned to his step. His eyes took on a friendly sparkle. When others spoke he listened. After all, he might be listening to the Messiah. When anyone asked for help, he responded; after all this might be the Messiah needing assistance.

The change of attitude was so significant that someone asked him why he was so happy. "I don't know," he answered. "All I know is that things changed when I started looking for God."

Now, that's curious. The old man saw Jesus because he didn't know what he looked like. The people in Jesus' day missed him because they thought they did.

How are things looking in your neighborhood?

A Gentle Thunder

*I*n the mystery of Christmas, we find
its majesty. The mystery of how God
became flesh, why he chose to come, and
how much he must love his people.

Such mysteries can never be solved, just as love
can never be diagrammed. Christmas is best
pondered, not with logic, but imagination.

—MAX LUCADO

The Christmas Child

The first Christmas was messy. Messy with crowded inns, traveling families, and barnyard animals sniffing at baby Jesus. Messy with questions: How did Mary become pregnant? What is Joseph supposed to tell his friends? Why is Herod hell-bent on killing babies?

Contrary to the tidy crèche on the front lawn, the first Christmas was chaotic: no midwife for Mary, no bed for Jesus, no explanation to give the scruffy shepherds who show up at midnight. The first Christmas was messy.

Is this one messy for you? Too many relatives? Or too much silence? First Christmas since the cemetery? Divorce? Pink slip? Christmas can be messy.

The next story describes one. But just as with Bethlehem, good came out of the mess. May good come out of yours.

I lowered my windshield visor, both to block the afternoon sun and retrieve the photo. With one hand holding the picture and the other on the steering wheel, I inched my rental car down Main Street.

Clearwater, Texas, was ready for Christmas. The sky was bright winter blue. A breeze just crisp enough for a jacket swayed the large plastic bells hanging beneath the lamp lights. Aluminum garlands connected the power poles, and Frosty the Snowman chased his hat on the Dairy Kreem window. Even the pickup truck in front of me had a wreath hanging on its tailgate. This central Texas town was ready for Christmas. But I wasn't.

I wanted to be back in Chicago. I wanted to be home. But things weren't so good at home. Meg and I had fought. Weeks of suppressed tension had exploded the day before. Same song, second verse.

"You promised to spend more time at home," she said.

"You promised not to nag," I replied.

She says I work too much. I say we've got bills to pay. She feels neglected. I feel frustrated. Finally, she told me we needed some—what was the word? Oh yeah, we needed some "space" . . . some time apart, and I agreed. I had an assignment in Dallas anyway, so why not go to Texas a few days early?

So, it was the fight with Meg that got me to Texas. But it was the photo that led me to Clearwater. My dad had received it in the mail. No return address. No letter. Just this photo: a black-and-white image of a large stone building. I could barely make out the words on the sign in front: Clearwater Lutheran Church.

Dad had no clue what the photo meant or who had sent it. We were familiar with the town, of course. Clearwater was where I was born and adopted. But we never lived there. My only previous visit had been when I was fresh out of college and curious. I had spent a day walking around asking questions, but that was twenty years ago. I hadn't been back since. And I wouldn't have returned now except Meg needed "space" and I could use an answer about the photo.

I pulled over to the side of the road and stopped in front of a two-story brick courthouse. Cardboard cutouts of Santa and his reindeer teetered on the lawn. I lowered my window and showed the photo to a couple of aging cowboys leaning against the side of a truck.

"Ever seen this place?" I asked.

They smiled at each other, and one cowboy spoke. "If you've got a strong arm, you could throw a rock from here and hit it."

He instructed me to turn right past the courthouse and turn right again. And when I did, I saw it. The church in the photo.

My preconceived notion of a small-town church didn't match what I was seeing. I had always imagined a small white-framed building with a simple belfry over the entrance. Something like an overgrown dollhouse. Not so, this structure. The white stone walls and tall steel roof spoke of permanence. Long wings extended to the right and left. I had expressed similar surprise when Dad first showed me the photo. But he had reminded me about the large number of German immigrants in the area—immigrants who took both their faith and their crafts seriously.

I parked in one of the diagonal spots near the church. In deference to the December chill, I put on my jacket, then grabbed my cap and gloves as I got out of the car. Tall elms canopied the wide sidewalk to the church steps. To my right was a brick sign bearing the name of the church in bronzed letters. On the left side of the church a nativity scene stood on the lawn. Although I didn't pause to examine it, I was impressed by its quality. Like the church, it seemed sturdy and detailed. I made a mental note to examine it later.

A sudden gust of wind at my back forced me to use two hands to pull open the thick wooden doors. Organ music welcomed me as I entered. With cap and gloves in hand, I stopped in the foyer. It was empty. From the look of things, it wouldn't be empty for long. The church had the appearance of a service about to happen. Large red and white poinsettias sat on the floor flanking the foyer doors. A guest book, open and ready to receive the names of visitors, rested on a podium. Garlands of pine looped across a large window that separated the foyer from the sanctuary.

I opened the doors and took a step inside. As I did, the volume of the organ music rose a notch. A long carpeted aisle bisected the auditorium, and a vaulted ceiling rose above it. Evening sunlight, tinted red by stained glass, cast long rectangles across the empty pews. An advent wreath hung on the pulpit, and unlit candles sat on the window sills. The only movements were those of a silver-haired woman rehearsing on the organ and an older fellow placing programs in hymnal racks. Neither noticed my entrance.

I spoke in the direction of the man. "Is there a service tonight?"

No response.

"Excuse me," I said a little louder. "Is there a service tonight?"

He looked up at me through wire-rimmed glasses, cocked his head, and cupped a hand behind his ear.

"I said, 'Is there a Christmas service tonight?!'" I felt awkward raising my voice in the sanctuary.

"No, we don't need a linen service, thank you. We wash our own towels."

I chuckled to myself, and when I did, I noticed how good it felt and how long it'd been. "No," I repeated, walking in his direction. "I was asking about the Christmas Eve service."

"Hold on." He turned toward the organist. "Sarah, can you hold up for a moment? We've got a salesman calling on us."

Sarah obliged, and the man looked at me again. "There now, what did you say?"

I repeated the question a fourth time.

"You planning to come?" he asked.

"I'm thinking about it."

"Good thing God was more convicted than you."

"What?"

"God didn't just give it thought, you know. He did it. He came."

Spunky, this guy. Short and square bodied. Not fat but barrel-chested. "Maintenance" was stenciled over the pocket of his gray shirt. He stepped out from the pews, walked up the aisle, and stood in front of me. As blue eyes sized me up, his stubby fingers scratched a thick crop of white hair.

"Been awhile since you've been in church?" His accent didn't sound pure Texan. Midwestern, maybe? I suppose I wasn't cloaking my discomfort too well. It had been awhile since I'd been in a church. And I did feel awkward being there, so I sidestepped the comment.

"I came because of this." I produced the photo. He looked down through his bifocals and smiled.

"My, the trees have grown." Looking up at me, he asked, "Where you from?"

"Chicago. I'm a journalist."

I don't always say that, but the old fellow seemed to be grading me, and I felt I could use a few points. If I earned any, he didn't say.

"You ought to be home for Christmas, son."

"Well, I'd like to, but I have an assignment and . . ."

"And your work has you out of town on Christmas Eve?"

Who are you to grill me? I started to ask, but didn't. Instead, I picked up a worship program and looked at it.

"Yeah, being home would be nice, but since I'm here I thought I'd . . ."

"Six o'clock."

"What?"

"The service. It starts at six." He extended a hand in my direction. "Joe's my name. Forgive me for being nosy. It's just that a man away from his wife . . ."

"How did you . . ."

"Your finger. I can see where your ring was. Must have been recent."

I looked at my hand and thumbed the line. Angry at Meg, I'd stuck my wedding band in my pocket on the plane. "Yeah, recent." I shrugged. "Listen, I'll be back at six. I'd like to meet the pastor. I've got some things to do now, though," I said, putting the program back in the hymnal rack.

"What a lie," I mumbled to myself as I turned. I had absolutely nothing to do and nowhere to go. Joe watched me as I walked down the aisle. At least I think he did. Only when I reached the foyer did I hear him whistling and working again. As I gave the auditorium one final look, Sarah resumed her rehearsal. I turned to go outside. The wooden doors were still stubborn. I paused on the steps, put on my cap, and looked around.

Several people stepped into the corner drugstore. *Last-minute shoppers*, I thought. A fellow with a western hat gave me a wave as he walked past. Not far behind him a woman clutching a shopping bag of gifts in one hand and a youngster's hand in the other scurried into the Smart Shoppe across the street. In the adjacent lot, cars encircled Happy's Cafe. Through snow-painted windows I could see families at the tables. I sighed at the sight of them, struck by the irony of my plight. All alone forty years ago. All alone today.

I took a deep breath and started down the steps, again noticing the manger scene to my right. Curious, I headed toward it, the yellow grass cracking beneath my feet as I walked.

Lowering my head, I entered the stable and studied the figures, obviously hand-carved, hand-painted. They were the largest ones I'd seen. The shepherds, though kneeling, were over two feet tall. I was struck by the extraordinary detail of the carvings. Joseph's beard wasn't just painted on; it was carved into the wood. His hand, resting on the manger, was complete with knuckles and fingernails. Mary knelt on the other side, her hand brushing hair back from her forehead as she looked at her son.

One shepherd had his hand on the shoulder of another. Their faces had a leather hue and a convincing look of awe. Even the wise men were unique, one gesturing at the infant, another holding the bridle of a camel, and the third reverently placing a gift before the crib.

Two cows dozed on folded legs. A sheep and three lambs occupied the space on the other side. I bent down and ran my hand over the white, varnished back of the smallest lamb.

"You won't find a set like this anywhere."

Startled, I stood and bumped my head on the roof of the stable. I turned. It was Joe. He'd donned a baseball cap and jacket.

"Each figure hand-carved," he continued, "right down to the last eyelash and hoof. Mr. Ottolman donated the manger scene to the church. It's been the pride of the city ever since."

"Mr. Autobahn?" I asked.

"Ottolman. A woodworker from Germany. This was his penance."

"Penance?"

"Self-imposed. He was drunk the night his wife went into labor. So drunk he wrecked the car while driving her to the hospital. The baby survived, but the mother didn't make it."

I squatted down and put my hand on Mary's face. I could feel the individual hairs of her eyebrows. Then I ran my finger across the smile on her lips.

"He spent the better part of a decade doing the work. He made a living building furniture and spent his time raising Carmen and carving these figures."

"Carmen was his daughter?"

"Yes, the girl who survived. Let me show you something."

Joe removed his hat, either out of reverence for the crèche or regard for the low roof, and knelt before the crib. I joined him. The grass was cold beneath our knees.

"Pull the blanket off the infant Jesus and look at his chest."

I did as he asked. Evening shadows made it difficult

to see, but I could make out the figure of a small cross furrowed into the wood. I ran my finger over the groove. Maybe a couple of inches long and half that wide, deep and wide enough for the tip of my finger.

"For nearly ten years a wooden scarlet cross sat in that space."

He could see the question on my face and explained. "Ottolman wasn't a believer when he began. But something about carving the face of the Messiah . . ." His voice drifted off for a minute as he touched the tiny chin. "Somewhere in the process he became interested. He went to church, this very church, and asked the pastor all about Jesus. Reverend Jackson told him not just about the birth but about the death of Christ and invited him to Sunday worship. He went.

"He took little Carmen with him. She was only a toddler. The two sat on the front pew and heard their first sermon. 'Born Crucified' was the name of the lesson. The message changed his life. He told everyone about it."

Joe smiled and stepped out from under the roof, then stood in the grass, his breath puffing clouds in the cold.

"He used to retell the message to Carmen every

night. He'd sit her on her bed and pretend he was the pastor." At this point Joe lowered his voice and took on a pulpit rhythm.

"'Baby Jesus was born to be crucified. He came not just for Bethlehem but for Calvary—not just to live with us but to die for us. Born with love in his eyes and the cross in his heart. He was born crucified.'"

Joe's blue eyes blazed, and his meaty fist punched the air, as if he were the reverend making the point.

"So you knew him?"

"I did."

"And Carmen?"

"Yes," he sighed. "Very well."

Still on my knees, I turned back to the baby and touched the indentation left by the cross. He chuckled behind me and said, "Ottolman told some of the members about his idea for the carving, and they thought it was crazy. 'Baby Jesus doesn't wear a cross,' they said. But he insisted. And one Christmas when he brought the figures out and set them on the lawn, there was a wooden scarlet cross in the baby's chest. Some people made a stink about it, but the reverend, he didn't mind."

"And the cross, where is it now? Is it lost?"

Joe put his hands in his pockets and stared off into space, then looked back at me. "No, it's not lost. Come with me." He turned and walked toward the church doors. I followed him into the building.

Over here," he called as I stood in the entrance, letting my eyes adjust to the darkening room.

I took off my cap, and Joe led me through a door off the right side of the foyer, down a long hall. We passed a row of portraits, apparently a gallery of pastors. I followed him around a corner until we stood in front of a door marked "Library." There must have been thirty keys hanging from a chain on Joe's belt. One of them unlocked the door. After he turned on the lights, we crossed the room to a corner where a stand held a thick scrapbook. In a couple of turns the old man found what he was looking for.

"This article appeared in our paper on Christmas Day, 1958."

The yellowed newsprint told the story:

STOLEN BABY JESUS HOME FOR CHRISTMAS

He was silent as I read the first paragraph.

"Mr. Ottolman must have been pretty angry."

"No, he wasn't upset."

"But his baby was taken."

"Finish the article, and I'll get us some coffee."

As he left the room, I continued reading:

The baby Jesus, part of a set hand-carved by a local woodworker, was taken from the Clearwater Lutheran Church sometime yesterday. The minister had posted a sign pleading for the babe's return. "At last night's Christmas Eve service," Reverend Jackson reported, "we had special prayers for the baby. With the homecoming of Baby Jesus, the prayers were answered."

I was staring at the photograph attached to the article when Joe returned with two Styrofoam cups of coffee. "Look closely," he said. "See anything missing?"

"The cross?"

Joe nodded. "Won't you sit down?"

We sat on either side of a long mahogany table. Joe took a sip of coffee and began.

"Nineteen fifty-eight. Carmen was eighteen. Lively, lovely girl, she was. Ottolman did his best to raise her, but she had her own ways. Would have been good had he remarried, but he never did.

"Told people a man only has room in his heart for one woman; Carmen was his. She was everything to him. Took her fishing on Saturdays and picked her up after school. Every Sunday the two sat on the front pew of this church and sang. My, how they sang.

"And every night he would pray. He'd thank God for his good grace and then beg God, 'Take care of my Carmen, Lord. Take care of my Carmen.'"

Joe looked away as if remembering her. For the first time I heard conversation in the hall. Parishioners were beginning to arrive. Somewhere a choir was rehearsing. Just as I found myself hoping Joe wouldn't stop his story, he continued. "Carmen's mother was a beauty from Mexico. And Carmen had every ounce of her beauty. Dark skin, black hair, and eyes that could melt your soul. She couldn't walk down Main Street without being whistled at.

"This bothered Ottolman. He was from the old school, you know. As she got older, he got stricter. It was for her own good, but she couldn't see that. He went too far, Ottolman did. He went too far. Told her to stay away from boys and to stay away from any place where boys were. And she did, mostly.

"Early in the summer of '58, Carmen discovered she was pregnant. She kept it from her father as long as she could. Being small of stature, she hid it quite well. But by December it was obvious. When he found out, he did something very, very bad. For the rest of his life he regretted that December night."

Joe's tone shifted from one of telling to one of questioning. "Why do people do the thing they swear they'll never do?"

I wasn't sure if he expected me to answer or not, but before I could, he sighed and continued.

"Well, Carmen's dad got mad and he got drunk. He wasn't a bad man; he just did a bad thing. He forgot his faith. And . . ."

Joe shook his head—"You're not going to believe this. Just before Christmas, he and Carmen had a wreck. Twice in one lifetime the man wrecked a car carrying the woman he loved."

Joe stopped again, I suppose to let me mull over

what he'd said. He was right; I found it hard to believe. How could a man repeat such a tragic event? But then, it occurred to me that I was doing the same with Meg.

Swearing to do better, only to fail again . . . and again. Maybe it wasn't so impossible after all.

"Go on," I urged. "What happened to them?"

"Ottolman came out of it okay, but Carmen was hurt, badly hurt. They took her to the hospital where her daddy sat by her bed every single minute. 'Oh, Jesus,' he would pray, 'take care of my Carmen. Don't let her die.' The doctors told him they would have to take the baby as soon as Carmen was stable.

"The night passed and Carmen slept. Ottolman sat by her side and Carmen slept. She slept right up until Christmas Eve morning. Then she woke up. Her first words were a question: 'Daddy, has my baby come?'

"He bounded out of his chair and took her hand. 'No, Carmen, but the baby is fine. The doctors are sure the baby is fine.'

"'Where am I?'

"He knelt at her bedside. 'You're in the hospital, darling. It's Christmas Eve.' He put her hand on his cheek and told her what had happened. He told her about his drinking and the accident and he began to weep. 'I'm so sorry, Carmen. I'm so sorry.'

"Then Carmen did a wonderful thing. She stroked her father's head and said, 'It's okay, Papa. It's okay. I love you.'

"He leaned forward and put his face in the crook of her neck and wept. Carmen cried too. She put her arm around her daddy's neck and cried.

"Neither said anything for the longest time; they just held each other, each tear washing away the hurt. Finally Carmen spoke: 'Papa, will the baby come before Christmas?'

"'I don't know, princess.'

"'I'd like that.' She smiled, her brown eyes twinkling. 'I'd like very much to have a baby to hold this Christmas Eve.'

"Those were her final words. She closed her eyes to rest. But she never woke up."

Joe's eyes misted, and he looked at the floor. I started to say he didn't have to tell me the rest of the story, but when he lifted his head, he was smiling—a soft, tender smile. "It was around lunchtime when Ottolman had the idea. 'You want to sleep with your baby, Carmen?' he whispered in her ear. 'I'll get you your baby.'

"For the first time in weeks he left the hospital. Out the door and across the street he marched. He walked straight past the courthouse and slowed his pace only when he neared the church. For a long time he stared at the crèche from across the street—the very crèche you saw this afternoon. He was planning something. He took a deep breath and crossed the church lawn.

"He began adjusting the manger scene, like he was inspecting the figures, looking for cracks or marks. Anyone passing by would have thought nothing of Mr. Ottolman examining his handiwork. And no one passing by would have seen that when he left, there was no baby Jesus in the manger.

"Only an hour later, when the reverend was showing the display to his grandchildren, did anyone notice. By then, the baby with the scarlet cross was wrapped in a blanket and nestled under the covers next to Carmen.

"Her final wish was granted. She held a baby on Christmas Eve."

For a long time neither Joe nor I spoke. He sat leaning forward, hands folded between his knees. He wasn't there. Nor was I. We were both in the world of Ottolman and Carmen and the sculptured baby in the manger. Though I'd never seen their faces, I could see them in my mind. I could see Ottolman pulling back the hospital sheets and placing the infant Jesus next to his daughter. And I could see him setting a chair next to the bed, taking Carmen's hand in his . . . and waiting.

I broke the silence with one word:

"Carmen?"

"She died two days later."

"The baby?"

"He came, early. But he came."

"Mr. Ottolman?"

"He stayed on in Clearwater. Still lives here, as a matter of fact. But he never went back to his house. He couldn't face the emptiness."

"So what happened to him?"

Joe cleared his throat. "Well, the church took him in—gave him a job and a little room at the back of the sanctuary."

Until that moment, until he spoke those words, the possibility had not entered my mind. I leaned forward and looked directly into his face. "Who are you?"

"You have her eyes, you know," he whispered.

"You mean, Carmen was . . ."

"Yes. Your mother. And I'm, well, I'm . . . your . . ."

". . . Grandfather?"

His chin began to tremble as he told me, "I've made some big mistakes, son. And I pray I'm not making another one right now. I just wanted you to know what happened. And I wanted to see you while I still could."

As I struggled to understand, he reached into his shirt pocket. He removed an object, placed it in my palm, and folded my hand around it. "I've been keeping this for you. She would want you to have it." And I opened my hand to see a cross—a small, wooden, scarlet cross.

Later that evening I called Meg from my room. I told her about Carmen, Ottolman, and the family I'd discovered. "Were you angry at Joe?" she asked.

"Funny," I said, "of all the emotions that flooded me

in that church library, anger wasn't one of them. Shock? Yes. Disbelief? Of course. But anger, no. Joe's assessment of himself sounds fair. He is a good man who did a very bad thing."

There was a long pause. Meg and I both knew what needed to be discussed next. She found a way to broach it. "What about me?" Her voice was soft. "Are you angry at me?"

With no hesitation, I responded, "No, there's been too much anger between us."

She agreed. "If Carmen forgave Joe, don't you suppose we could do the same for each other?"

"I'll be home tomorrow," I told my wife.

"I've got a better idea," she replied.

So Meg flew to Texas to be with us. She made it to Clearwater in time to have dinner with two men who, by virtue of mistakes and mercy and Christmas miracles, had found their way home for the holidays.

*O*h, the things we do to give gifts to those we love.

But we don't mind, do we? We would do it all again.
Fact is, we *do* it all again. Every Christmas, every
birthday, every so often we find ourselves in foreign
territory. Grownups are in toy stores, dads are in
teen stores. Wives are in the hunting department,
and husbands are in the purse department.

Not only do we enter unusual places, we do unusual
things. We assemble bicycles at midnight. We hide the
new tires with mag wheels under the stairs. One fellow
I heard about rented a movie theater so he and his wife
could see their wedding pictures on their anniversary.

And we'd do it all again. Having pressed the grapes
of service, we drink life's sweetest wine—the wine
of giving. We are at our best when we are giving. In
fact, we are most like God when we are giving.

He Chose the Nails

God Guides
the Wise

*H*oliday time is highway time. Ever since the magi packed their bags for Bethlehem, the birth of Jesus has caused people to hit the road. Our Christmas trips have a lot in common with the one of the wise men. We don't camp with camels, but we have been known to bump into a knobby-kneed in-law on the way to the bathroom. We don't keep an eye out for star lights, but flashing lights of the highway patrol? We watch for them at every curve. And we don't ride in a spice-road caravan, but six hours in a minivan with four kids might have made the wise men thankful for animals.

It's not always ho ho ho on the high, high highway.

Extended time in the car reveals human frailties.

Dads refuse to stop. They hearken back to the examples of their forefathers. Did the pioneers spend the night at a Holiday Inn? Did Lewis and Clark ask for directions? Did Joseph allow Mary to stroll through a souvenir shop on the road to Bethlehem? By no means. Men drive as if they have a biblical mandate to travel far and fast, stopping only for gasoline.

And children? Road trips do to kids what a full moon does to the wolf man. If one child says, "I like that song," you might expect the other to say, "That's nice." Won't happen. Instead the other child will reply, "It stinks and so do your feet."

There is also the issue of JBA—juvenile bladder activity. A child can go weeks without going to the bathroom at home. But once on the road, the kid starts leaking like secrets in Washington. On one drive to Colorado, my daughters visited every toilet in New Mexico.

The best advice for traveling with young children is

to be thankful they aren't teenagers. Teens are embarrassed by what their parents say, think, wear, eat, and sing. So for their sakes (and if you ever want to see your future grandchildren), don't smile at the waitstaff, don't breathe, and don't sing with the window down or up.

It's wiser to postpone traveling with children until they are a more reasonable age—like forty-two.

Christmas and travel. The first has a way of prompting the second and has done so ever since the delegation from the distant land came searching for Jesus.

> Jesus was born in Bethlehem in Judea, during the reign of King Herod. About that time some wise men from eastern lands arrived in Jerusalem, asking,
>
> "Where is the newborn king of the Jews?" (Matt. 2:1–2 NLT)

Matthew loved the magi. He gave their story more square inches of text than he gave the narrative of the birth of Jesus. He never mentions the shepherds or the manger, but he didn't want us to miss the star and the seekers. It's easy to see why. Their story is our story. We're all travelers, all sojourners. In order to find Jesus, every

147

one of us needs direction. God gives it. The story of the wise men shows us how.

> We have seen His star in the East and have come to worship Him. (v. 2 NKJV)

God uses the natural world to get our attention. Earth and stars form the first missionary society. "The heavens declare the glory of God" (Ps. 19:1 NKJV). As Paul wrote, "The basic reality of God is plain enough. Open your eyes and there it is! By taking a long and thoughtful look at what God has created, people have always been able to see what their eyes as such can't see: eternal power, for instance, and the mystery of his divine being" (Rom. 1:19–20 MSG).

God led the wise men to Jerusalem with a star. But to lead them to Jesus, he used something else:

> King Herod was deeply disturbed when he heard this, as was everyone in Jerusalem. He called a meeting of the leading priests and teachers of religious law and asked, "Where is the Messiah supposed to be born?"

"In Bethlehem in Judea," they said, "for this is what the prophet wrote:

'And you, O Bethlehem in the land of Judah,
are not least among the ruling cities of Judah,
for a ruler will come from you
who will be the shepherd for my people Israel.'"

(MATT. 2:3–6 NLT)

The star sign was enough to lead the magi to Jerusalem.

But it took Scripture to lead them to Jesus.

People see signs of God every day. Sunsets that steal the breath. Newborns that bring tears. Migrating geese that stir a smile. But do all who see the signs draw near to God? No. Many are content simply to see the signs. They do not realize that the riches of God are intended to turn us toward him. "Perhaps you do not understand that God is kind to you so you will change your hearts and lives" (Rom. 2:4 NCV).

The wise men, however, understood the purpose of the sign.

They followed it to Jerusalem, where they heard

about the scripture. The prophecy told them where to find Christ. It is interesting to note that the star reappeared *after* they learned about the prophecy. The star "came and stood shining *right over* the place where the Child was" (Matt. 2:9, emphasis mine).[1] It is as if the sign and word worked together to bring the wise men to Jesus. The ultimate aim of all God's messages, both miraculous and written, is to shed the light of heaven on Jesus.

> They came to the house where the child was and saw him with his mother, Mary, and they bowed down and worshiped him. They opened their gifts and gave him treasures of gold, frankincense, and myrrh. (v. 11 NCV)

Behold the first Christian worshippers. The simple dwelling became a cathedral. Seekers of Christ found him and knelt in his presence. They gave him gifts: gold for a king, frankincense for a priest, and myrrh for his burial.

They found the Christ because they heeded the sign and believed the scripture.

---

1. Frederick Dale Bruner, *Matthew: A Commentary*, vol. 1, *The Christbook: Matthew 1–12*, rev. and exp. ed. (Grand Rapids: William B. Eerdmans, 2004), 60.

Noticeably absent at the manger were the scholars of the Torah. They reported to Herod that the Messiah would be born in Bethlehem. Did they not read the prophecy? Yes, but they did not respond to it. You'd think at a minimum they would have accompanied the magi to Bethlehem. The village was near enough. The risk was small enough. At worst they would be out the effort. At best they would see the fulfillment of prophecy. But the priests showed no interest.

The wise men earned their moniker because they did. Their hearts were open to God's gift. The men were never the same again. After worshipping the Christ child, "they departed for their own country another way" (v. 12 NKJV). Matthew uses the word *way* in other places to suggest a direction of life. He speaks of the narrow way (7:13–14 NASB) and "the way of righteousness" (21:32). He may be telling us that the wise men went home as different men.

Called by a sign. Instructed by Scripture. And directed home by God.

It's as if all the forces of heaven cooperated to guide the wise men.

God uses every possible means to communicate with

you. The wonders of nature call to you. The promises and prophecies of Scripture speak to you. God himself reaches out to you. He wants to help you find your way home.

Many years ago I watched the television adaptation of the drama *The Miracle Worker*, the compelling story of two females with great resolve: Helen Keller and Anne Sullivan. Helen was born in 1880. She wasn't yet two when she contracted an illness that left her blind, deaf, and mute. When Helen was seven years old, Annie, a young, partially blind teacher, came to the Kellers' Alabama home to serve as Helen's teacher.

Helen's brother James tried to convince Annie to quit. The teacher wouldn't consider it. She was resolved to help Helen function in a world of sight and sound. Helen was as stubborn as her teacher. Locked in a frightening, lonely world, she misinterpreted Annie's attempts. The result was a battle of wills. Over and over Annie pressed sign language into Helen's palm. Helen pulled back. Annie persisted. Helen resisted.

Finally, in a moment of high drama, a breakthrough. During a fevered exchange near the water pump, Annie placed one of Helen's hands under the spout of flowing water. Into the other hand she spelled out w-a-t-e-r. Over and over, w-a-t-e-r. Helen pulled back. Annie kept signing. W-a-t-e-r.

All of a sudden Helen stopped. She placed her hand on her teacher's and repeated the letters w-a-t-e-r. Annie beamed. She lifted Helen's hand onto her own cheek and nodded vigorously. "Yes, yes, yes! W-a-t-e-r." Helen spelled it again: w-a-t-e-r. Helen pulled Annie around the yard, spelling out the words. G-r-o-u-n-d. P-o-r-c-h. P-u-m-p. It was a victory parade.[2]

Christmas celebrates a similar moment for us—God breaking through to our world. In a feeding stall of all places. He will not leave us in the dark. He is the pursuer, the teacher. He won't sit back while we miss out. So he entered our world. He sends signals and messages: H-o-p-e. L-i-f-e. He cracks the shell of our world and invites us to peek into his. And every so often a seeking soul looks up.

May you be one of them.

When God sends signs, be faithful. Let them lead you to Scripture.

---

2. "Water Scene," *The Miracle Worker*, directed by Paul Aaron (1979; Atlanta, GA: Half-Pint Productions).

As Scripture directs, be humble. Let it lead you to worship.

And as you worship the Son, be grateful. He will lead you home. Who knows? Perhaps before Jesus comes again, we'll discover why men don't ask for directions. Then we can pursue the other great question of life: Why do women apply makeup while they are driving?

But that's a question for ones wiser than I.

BECAUSE OF BETHLEHEM

The Answer
Is Yes

*F*ive-year-old Madeline climbed into her father's lap.

"Did you have enough to eat?" he asked her.

She smiled and patted her tummy. "I can't eat any more."

"Did you have some of your grandma's pie?"

"A whole piece!"

Joe looked across the table at his mom. "Looks like you filled us up. Don't think we'll be able to do anything tonight but go to bed."

Madeline put her little hands on either side of his big face. "Oh, but, Poppa, this is Christmas Eve. You said we could dance."

Joe feigned a poor memory. "Did I now? Why, I don't remember saying anything about dancing."

Grandma smiled and shook her head as she began clearing the table.

"But, Poppa," Madeline pleaded, "we always dance on Christmas Eve. Just you and me, remember?"

A smile burst from beneath his thick mustache. "Of course I remember, darling. How could I forget?"

And with that he stood and took her hand in his, and for a moment, just a moment, his wife was alive again, and the two were walking into the den to spend another night before Christmas as they had spent so many, dancing away the evening.

They would have danced the rest of their lives, but then came the surprise pregnancy and the complications. Madeline survived. But her mother did not. And Joe, the thick-handed butcher from Minnesota, was left to raise his Madeline alone.

"Come on, Poppa." She tugged on his hand. "Let's dance before everyone arrives." She was right. Soon the doorbell would ring and the relatives would fill the floor and the night would be past.

But, for now, it was just Poppa and Madeline.

Rebellion flew into Joe's world like a Minnesota blizzard. About the time she was old enough to drive, Madeline decided she was old enough to lead her life. And that life did not include her father.

"I should have seen it coming," Joe would later say, "but for the life of me I didn't." He didn't know what to do. He didn't know how to handle the pierced nose and the tight shirts. He didn't understand the late nights and the poor grades. And, most of all, he didn't know when to speak and when to be quiet.

She, on the other hand, had it all figured out. She knew when to speak to her father—never. She knew when to be quiet—always. The pattern was reversed, however, with the lanky, tattooed kid from down the street. He was no good, and Joe knew it.

And there was no way he was going to allow his daughter to spend Christmas Eve with that kid.

"You'll be with us tonight, young lady. You'll be at your grandma's house eating your grandma's pie. You'll be with us on Christmas Eve."

Though they were at the same table, they might as well have been on different sides of town. Madeline played with her food and said nothing. Grandma tried to talk to Joe, but he was in no mood to chat. Part of him was angry; part of him was heartbroken. And the rest of him would have given anything to know how to talk to this girl who once sat on his lap.

Soon the relatives arrived, bringing with them a welcome end to the awkward silence. As the room filled with noise and people, Joe stayed on one side, Madeline sat sullenly on the other.

"Put on the music, Joe," reminded one of his brothers. And so he did. Thinking she would be honored, he turned and walked toward his daughter. "Will you dance with your poppa tonight?"

The way she huffed and turned, you'd have thought he'd insulted her. In full view of the family, she walked out the front door and marched down the sidewalk. Leaving her father alone.

Very much alone.

Madeline came back that night but not for long. Joe never faulted her for leaving. After all, what's it like being the daughter of a butcher? In their last days together he tried so hard. He made her favorite dinner—she didn't want to eat. He invited her to a movie—she stayed in her room. He bought her a new dress—she didn't even say thank you. And then there was that spring day he left work early to be at the house when she arrived home from school.

Wouldn't you know that was the day she never came home.

A friend saw her and her boyfriend in the vicinity of the bus station. The authorities confirmed the purchase of a ticket to Chicago; where she went from there was anybody's guess.

※

The scrawny boy with the tattoos had a cousin. The cousin worked the night shift at a convenience store south of Houston. For a few bucks a month, he would let the runaways stay in his apartment at night, but they had to be out during the day.

Which was fine with them. They had big plans. He was going to be a mechanic, and Madeline just knew she could get a job at a department store. Of course he knew nothing about cars, and she knew even less about getting a job—but you don't think of things like that when you're intoxicated on freedom.

After a couple of weeks, the cousin changed his mind. And the day he announced his decision, the boyfriend announced his. Madeline found herself facing the night with no place to sleep or hand to hold.

It was the first of many such nights.

A woman in the park told her about the homeless shelter near the bridge. For a couple of bucks she could get a bowl of soup and a cot. A couple of bucks was about all she had. She used her backpack as a pillow and jacket as a blanket. The room was so rowdy it was hard to sleep. Madeline turned her face to the wall and, for the first time in several days, thought of the whiskered face of her father as he would kiss her good night. But as her eyes began to water, she refused to cry. She pushed the memory deep inside and determined not to think about home.

She'd gone too far to go back.

The next morning the girl in the cot beside her showed her a fistful of tips she'd made from dancing on tables. "This is the last night I'll have to stay here," she said. "Now I can pay for my own place. They told me they are looking for another girl. You should come by."

She reached into her pocket and pulled out a matchbook. "Here's the address."

Madeline's stomach turned at the thought. All she could do was mumble, "I'll think about it."

She spent the rest of the week on the streets looking for work. At the end of the week, when it was time to pay her bill at the shelter, she reached into her pocket and pulled out the matchbook. It was all she had left.

"I won't be staying tonight," she said, and walked out the door.

Hunger has a way of softening convictions.

❦

If Madeline knew anything, she knew how to dance. Her father had taught her. Now men the age of her father watched her. She didn't rationalize it—she just didn't think about it. Madeline simply did her work and took their dollars.

She might have never thought about it, except for the letters. The cousin brought them. Not one, or two, but a box full. All addressed to her. All from her father.

"Your old boyfriend must have squealed on you.

These come two or three a week," complained the cousin. "Give him your address." Oh, but she couldn't do that. He might find her.

Nor could she bear to open the envelopes. She knew what they said; he wanted her home. But if he knew what she was doing, he would not be writing.

It seemed less painful not to read them. So she didn't. Not that week, nor the next when the cousin brought more, nor the next when he came again. She kept them in the dressing room at the club, organized according to postmark. She ran her finger over the top of each but couldn't bring herself to open one.

Most days Madeline was able to numb the emotions. Thoughts of home and thoughts of shame were shoved into the same part of her heart. But there were occasions when the thoughts were too strong to resist.

Like the time she saw a dress in the clothing store window. A dress the same color as one her father had purchased for her. A dress that had been far too plain for her. With much reluctance she had put it on and stood with him before the mirror. "My, you are as tall as I am," he had told her. She had stiffened at his touch.

Seeing her weary face reflected in the store window,

Madeline realized she'd give a thousand dresses to feel his arm again. She left the store and resolved not to pass by it again.

In time the leaves fell and the air chilled. The mail came and the cousin complained and the stack of letters grew. Still she refused to send him an address. And she refused to read a letter.

Then a few days before Christmas Eve another letter arrived. Same shape. Same color. But this one had no postmark. And it was not delivered by the cousin. It was sitting on her dressing room table.

"A couple of days ago a big man stopped by and asked me to give this to you," explained one of the other dancers. "Said you'd understand the message."

"He was here?" she asked anxiously.

The woman shrugged, "Suppose he had to be."

Madeline swallowed hard and looked at the envelope. She opened it and removed the card. "I know where you are," it read. "I know what you do. This doesn't change the way I feel. What I've said in each letter is still true."

"But I don't know what you've said," Madeline declared. She pulled a letter from the top of the stack and read it. Then a second and a third. Each letter had the same sentence. Each sentence asked the same question.

In a matter of moments the floor was littered with paper and her face was streaked with tears.

Within an hour she was on a bus. "I just might make it in time."

She barely did.

The relatives were starting to leave. Joe was helping grandma in the kitchen when his brother called from the suddenly quiet den. "Joe, someone is here to see you."

Joe stepped out of the kitchen and stopped. In one hand the girl held a backpack. In the other she held a card. Joe saw the question in her eyes.

"The answer is 'yes,'" she said to her father. "If the invitation is still good, the answer is 'yes.'"

Joe swallowed hard. "Oh my. The invitation is good."

And so the two danced again on Christmas Eve.

On the floor, near the door, rested a letter with Madeline's name and her father's request.

"Will you come home and dance with your poppa again?"

HE CHOSE THE NAILS

God sent more than miracles
and messages. He sent his Son.

—MAX LUCADO

The North Pole
or the Manger?

*S*ome call him Sinterklaas. Others Pere Noel or Papa Noel. He's been known as Hoteiosho, Sonnerklaas, Father Christmas, Jelly Belly, and to most English speakers, Santa Claus.

His original name was Nicholas, which means victorious. He was born in AD 280 in what is now Turkey. He was orphaned at age nine when his parents died of a plague. Though many would think Santa majored in toy making and minored in marketing, actually the original Nicholas studied Greek philosophy and Christian doctrine.

He was honored by the Catholic Church by being named Bishop of Myra in the early fourth century. He held the post until his death on December 6, 343.

History recognized him as a saint, but in the third century he was a bit of a troublemaker. He was twice jailed, once by the Emperor Diocletian for religious reasons, the other for slugging a fellow bishop during a fiery debate. (So much for finding out who is naughty and nice.)

Old Nick never married. But that's not to say he wasn't a romantic. He was best known for the kindness he showed to a poor neighbor who was unable to support his three daughters or provide the customary dowry so they could attract husbands. Old Saint Nicholas slipped up to the house by night and dropped a handful of gold coins through the window so the eldest daughter could afford to get married. He repeated this act on two other nights for the other two daughters.

This story was the seed that, watered with years, became the Santa legend. It seems that every generation adorned it with another ornament until it sparkled more than a Christmas tree.

The gift grew from a handful of coins to bags of

coins. Instead of dropping them through the window, he dropped them down the chimney. And rather than land on the floor, the bags of coins landed in the girls' stockings, which were hanging on the hearth to dry. (So that's where all this stocking stuff started.)

The centuries have been as good to Nicholas's image as to his deeds. Not only have his acts been embellished, his wardrobe and personality have undergone transformations as well.

As Bishop of Myra, he wore the traditional ecclesiastical robes and a mitered hat. He is known to have been slim, with a dark beard and a serious personality.

By 1300 he was wearing a white beard. By the 1800s he was depicted with a rotund belly and an ever-present basket of food over his arm. Soon came the black boots, a red cape, and a cheery stocking on his head. In the late nineteenth century his basket of food became a sack of toys. In 1866 he was small and gnomish but by 1930 he was a robust six-footer with rosy cheeks and a Coca-Cola.

Santa reflects the desires of people all over the world. With the centuries he has become the composite of what we want:

A friend who cares enough to travel a long way against all odds to bring good gifts to good people.

A sage who, though aware of each act, has a way of rewarding the good and overlooking the bad.

A friend of children, who never gets sick and never grows old.

A father who lets you sit on his lap and share your deepest desires.

Santa. The culmination of what we need in a hero. The personification of our passions. The expression of our yearnings. The fulfillment of our desires.

And . . . the betrayal of our meager expectations.

What? you say. Let me explain.

You see, Santa can't provide what we really need. For one thing, he's only around once a year. When January winds chill our souls, he's history. When December's requests become February payments, Santa's left the mall. When April demands taxes or May brings final exams, Santa is still months from his next visit. And should July find us ill or October find us alone, we can't go to his chair for comfort—it's still empty. He only comes once a year.

And when he comes, though he gives much, he

doesn't take away much. He doesn't take away the riddle of the grave, the burden of mistakes, or the anxiety of demands. He's kind and quick and cute; but when it comes to healing hurts—don't go to Santa.

Now, I don't mean to be a Scrooge. I'm not wanting to slam the jolly old fellow. I am just pointing out that we people are timid when it comes to designing legends.

You'd think we could do better. You'd think that over six centuries we'd develop a hero who'd resolve those fears.

But we can't. We have made many heroes, from King Arthur to Kennedy; Lincoln to Lindbergh; Socrates to Santa to Superman. We give it the best we can, every benefit of every doubt, every supernatural strength, and for a brief shining moment we have the hero we need— the king who can deliver Camelot. But then the truth leaks, and fact surfaces amid the fiction, and the chinks in the armor are seen. And we realize that the heroes, as noble as they may have been, as courageous as they were, were conceived in the same stained society as you and I.

Except one. There was one who claimed to come from a different place. There was one who, though he had the appearance of a man, claimed to have the origin of God. There was one who, while wearing the face of a Jew, had the image of the Creator.

Those who saw him—really saw him—knew there was something different. At his touch blind beggars saw. At his command crippled legs walked. At his embrace empty lives filled with vision.

He fed thousands with one basket. He stilled a storm with one command. He raised the dead with one proclamation. He changed lives with one request. He rerouted the history of the world with one life, lived in one country, was born in one manger, and died on one hill . . .

After three years of ministry, hundreds of miles, thousands of miracles, innumerable teachings, Jesus asks, "Who?" Jesus bids the people to ponder not what he has done but who he is.

It's the ultimate question of the Christ: Whose son is he?

Is he the son of God or the sum of our dreams? Is he the force of creation or a figment of our imagination?

When we ask that question about Santa, the answer is the culmination of our desires. A depiction of our fondest dreams.

Not so when we ask it about Jesus. For no one could ever dream a person as incredible as he is. The idea that a virgin would be selected by God to bear himself . . . The notion that God would don a scalp and toes and two eyes . . . The thought that the King of the universe would sneeze and burp and get bit by mosquitoes . . . It's too incredible. Too revolutionary. We would never create such a Savior. We aren't that daring.

When we create a redeemer, we keep him safely distant in his faraway castle. We allow him only the briefest of encounters with us. We permit him to swoop in and out with his sleigh before we can draw too near. We wouldn't ask him to take up residence in the midst of a contaminated people. In our wildest imaginings we wouldn't conjure a king who becomes one of us.

But God did. God did what we wouldn't dare dream. He did what we couldn't imagine. He became a man so we could trust him. He became a sacrifice so we could know him. And he defeated death so we could follow him.

It defies logic. It is a divine insanity. A holy incredibility. Only a God beyond systems and common sense could create a plan as absurd as this. Yet it is the very impossibility of it all that makes it possible. The wildness of the story is its strongest witness.

For only a God could create a plan this mad. Only a Creator beyond the fence of logic could offer such a gift of love.

What man can't do, God does.

So, when it comes to goodies and candy, cherub cheeks and red noses, go to the North Pole.

But when it comes to eternity, forgiveness, purpose, and truth, go to the manger. Kneel with the shepherds. Worship the God who dared to do what man dared not dream.

AND THE ANGELS WERE SILENT

Christ Is Born

$\mathcal{G}$od did something extraordinary.

Stepping from the throne, he removed his robe
of light and wrapped himself in skin: pigmented,
human skin. The light of the universe entered a
dark, wet womb. He whom angels worship nestled
himself in the placenta of a peasant, was birthed
into a cold night, and then slept on cow's hay.

Mary didn't know whether to give him milk or
give him praise, but she gave him both since he
was, as near as she could figure, hungry and holy.

Joseph didn't know whether to call him Junior
or Father. But in the end he called him Jesus,
since that's what the angel had said and since
he didn't have the faintest idea what to name
a God he could cradle in his arms . . .

IN THE GRIP OF GRACE

Gabriel's
Questions

*G*abriel must have scratched his head at this one.

He wasn't one to question his God-given missions. Sending fire and dividing seas were all in an eternity's work for this angel. When God sent, Gabriel went.

And when word got out that God was to become man, Gabriel was enthused. He could envision the moment:

The Messiah in a blazing chariot.

The King descending on a fiery cloud.

An explosion of light from which the Messiah would emerge.

That's what he expected. What he never expected, however, was what he got: a slip of paper with a Nazarene address. "God will become a baby," it read. "Tell the mother to name the child Jesus. And tell her not to be afraid."

Gabriel was never one to question, but this time he had to wonder.

God will become a baby? Gabriel had seen babies before. He had been platoon leader on the bulrush operation. He remembered what little Moses looked like.

That's okay for humans, he thought to himself. *But God?*

The heavens can't contain him; how could a body? Besides, have you seen what comes out of those babies? Hardly befitting for the Creator of the universe. Babies must be carried and fed, bounced and bathed. To imagine some mother burping God on her shoulder—why, that was beyond what even an angel could imagine.

And what of this name—what was it—Jesus? Such a common name. There's a Jesus in every cul-de-sac. Come on, even Gabriel has more punch to it than Jesus. Call the baby Eminence or Majesty or Heaven-sent. Anything but Jesus.

So Gabriel scratched his head. What happened to the good ol' days? The Sodom and Gomorrah stuff. Flooding the globe. Flaming swords. That's the action he liked.

But Gabriel had his orders. Take the message to Mary. Must be a special girl, he assumed as he traveled. But Gabriel was in for another shock. One peek told him Mary was no queen. The mother-to-be of God was not regal. She was a Jewish peasant who'd barely outgrown her acne and had a crush on a guy named Joe.

And speaking of Joe—what does this fellow know? Might as well be a weaver in Spain or a cobbler in Greece. He's a carpenter. Look at him over there, sawdust in his beard and nail apron around his waist. You're telling me God is going to have dinner every night with him? You're telling me the source of wisdom is going to call this guy "Dad"? You're telling me a common laborer is going to be charged with giving food to God?

What if he gets laid off?

What if he gets cranky?

What if he decides to run off with a pretty young girl from down the street? Then where will we be?

It was all Gabriel could do to keep from turning

back. "This is a peculiar idea you have, God," he must have muttered to himself.

Are God's guardians given to such musings?

Are we?

WHEN GOD WHISPERS YOUR NAME

God loved us too much
to leave us alone.

—MAX LUCADO

The Night in
the Stable

*M*atthew describes Jesus' earthly father as a crafts-man (Matt. 13:55). A small-town carpenter, he lives in Nazareth: a single-camel map dot on the edge of boredom. Is he the right choice? Doesn't God have better options? An eloquent priest from Jerusalem or a scholar from the Pharisees? Why Joseph? A major part of the answer lies in his reputation: he gives it up for Jesus. "Then Joseph [Mary's] husband, being a just man, and not wanting to make her a public example, was minded to put her away secretly" (Matt. 1:19 NKJV).

With the phrase "a just man," Matthew recognizes the status of Joseph. Nazareth viewed him as we might view an elder, deacon, or Bible class teacher. Joseph likely took pride in his standing, but Mary's announcement jeopardized it: I'm pregnant.

Now what? His fiancée is blemished, tainted . . . He is righteous, godly. On one hand, he has the law. On the other, he has his love. The law says, stone her. Love says, forgive her. Joseph is caught in the middle.

Then comes the angel. Mary's growing belly gives no cause for concern but reason to rejoice. "She carries the Son of God in her womb," the angel announces. But who would believe it?

A bead of sweat forms beneath Joseph's beard. He faces a dilemma. Make up a lie and preserve his place in the community or tell the truth and kiss his reputation good-bye. He makes his decision. "Joseph . . . took to him his wife, and did not know her till she had brought forth her firstborn Son" (Matt. 1:24–25 NKJV).

Joseph swapped his Torah studies for a pregnant fiancée and an illegitimate son and made the big decision of discipleship. He placed God's plan ahead of his own.

Which makes me think about knotholes and

snapshots and "I wonders." You'll find them in every chapter of the Bible about every person. But nothing stirs so many questions as does the birth of Christ. Characters appear and disappear before we can ask them anything. The innkeeper too busy to welcome God—did he ever learn who he turned away? The shepherds—did they ever hum the song the angels sang? The wise men who followed the star—what was it like to worship a toddler? And Joseph, especially Joseph. I've got questions for Joseph.

Did you and Jesus arm wrestle? Did he ever let you win?

Did you ever look up from your prayers and see Jesus listening?

How do you say "Jesus" in Egyptian?

What ever happened to the wise men?

What ever happened to you?

We don't know what happened to Joseph. His role in Act I is so crucial that we expect to see him the rest of the drama—but with the exception of a short scene with twelve-year-old Jesus in Jerusalem, he never reappears. The rest of his life is left to speculation, and we are left with our questions.

But of all my questions, my first would be about Bethlehem. I'd like to know about the night in the stable. I can picture Joseph there. Moonlit pastures. Stars twinkle above. Bethlehem sparkles in the distance. There he is, pacing outside the stable.

What was he thinking while Jesus was being born? What was on his mind while Mary was giving birth? He'd done all he could do—heated the water, prepared a place for Mary to lie. He'd made Mary as comfortable as she could be in a barn, and then he stepped out. She'd asked to be alone, and Joseph has never felt more so.

In that eternity between his wife's dismissal and Jesus' arrival, what was he thinking? He walked into the night and looked into the stars. Did he pray?

For some reason, I don't see him silent; I see Joseph animated, pacing. Head shaking one minute, fist shaking the next. This isn't what he had in mind. I wonder what he said . . .

This isn't the way I planned it, God. Not at all. My child being born in a stable? This isn't the way I thought it would be. A cave with sheep and donkeys, hay and straw? My wife giving birth with only the stars to hear her pain?

This isn't at all what I imagined. No, I imagined family. I imagined grandmothers. I imagined neighbors clustered outside the door and friends standing at my side. I imagined the house erupting with the first cry of the infant. Slaps on the back. Loud laughter. Jubilation.

That's how I thought it would be.

The midwife would hand me my child, and all the people would applaud. Mary would rest and we would celebrate. All of Nazareth would celebrate.

But now. Now look. Nazareth is five days' journey away. And here we are in a . . . in a sheep pasture. Who will celebrate with us? The sheep? The shepherds? The stars?

This doesn't seem right. What kind of husband am I? I provide no midwife to aid my wife. No bed to rest her back. Her pillow is a blanket from my donkey. My house for her is a shed of hay and straw.

The smell is bad, the animals are loud. Why, I even smell like a shepherd myself.

Did I miss something? Did I, God?

When you sent the angel and spoke of the son being born—this isn't what I pictured. I envisioned Jerusalem, the temple, the priests, and the people gathered to watch. A pageant perhaps. A parade. A banquet at least. I mean, this is the Messiah!

Or, if not born in Jerusalem, how about Nazareth? Wouldn't Nazareth have been better? At least there I have my house and my business. Out here, what do I have? A weary mule, a stack of firewood, and a pot of warm water. This is not the way I wanted it to be! This is not the way I wanted my son.

Oh my, I did it again. I did it again, didn't I, Father? I don't mean to do that; it's just that I forget. He's not my son . . . He's yours.

The child is yours. The plan is yours. The idea is yours. And forgive me for asking but . . . is this how God enters the world? The coming of the angel, I've accepted. The questions people asked about the pregnancy, I can tolerate. The trip to Bethlehem, fine. But why a birth in a stable, God?

Any minute now Mary will give birth. Not to a child, but to the Messiah. Not to an infant, but to God. That's what the angel said. That's what Mary believes.

And, God, my God, that's what I want to believe. But surely you can understand; it's not easy. It seems so . . . so . . . so . . . bizarre.

I'm unaccustomed to such strangeness, God. I'm a carpenter. I make things fit. I square off the edges. I follow the plumb line. I measure twice before I cut once. Surprises are not the friend of a builder. I like to know the plan. I like to see the plan before I begin.

But this time I'm not the builder, am I? This time I'm a tool. A hammer in your grip. A nail between your fingers. A chisel in your hands. This project is yours, not mine.

I guess it's foolish of me to question you. Forgive my struggling. Trust doesn't come easy to me, God. But you never said it would be easy, did you?

One final thing, Father. The angel you sent? Any chance you could send another? If not an angel, maybe a person? I don't know anyone around here and some company would be nice. Maybe the innkeeper or a traveler? Even a shepherd would do.

I wonder. Did Joseph ever pray such a prayer?

CURE FOR THE COMMON LIFE AND *HE STILL MOVES STONES*

*L*ove goes the distance . . . and Christ traveled
from limitless eternity to be confined by time
in order to become one of us. He didn't have
to. He could have given up. At any step along
the way he could have called it quits.

When he saw the size of the womb,
he could have stopped.

When he saw how tiny his hand would be, how soft
his voice would be, how hungry his tummy would
be, he could have stopped. At the first whiff of the
stinky stable, at the first gust of cold air. The first
time he scraped his knee or blew his nose or tasted
burnt bagels, he could have turned and walked out.

But he didn't.

He didn't, because he is love.

A LOVE WORTH GIVING

No Room in
the Inn

The noise and the bustle began earlier than usual in the village. As night gave way to dawn, people were already on the streets. Vendors were positioning themselves on the corners of the most heavily traveled avenues. Store owners were unlocking the doors to their shops. Children were awakened by the excited barking of the street gods and the complaints of donkeys pulling carts.

The owner of the inn had awakened earlier than most in the town. After all, the inn was full, all the beds taken. Every available mat or blanket had been put to use. Soon all the customers would be stirring, and there would be a lot of work to do.

One's imagination is kindled thinking about the conversation of the innkeeper and his family at the breakfast table. Did anyone mention the arrival of the young couple the night before? Did anyone ask about their welfare? Did anyone comment on the pregnancy of the girl on the donkey? Perhaps. Perhaps someone raised the subject. But, at best, it was raised, not discussed. There was nothing *that* novel about them. They were, possibly, one of several families turned away that night.

Besides, who had time to talk about them when there was so much excitement in the air? Augustus did the economy of Bethlehem a favor when he decreed that a census should be taken. Who could remember when such commerce had hit the village?

No, it was doubtful that anyone mentioned the couple's arrival or wondered about the condition of the girl. They were too busy. The day was upon them. The day's bread had to be made. The morning's chores had to be done. There was too much to do to imagine that the impossible had occurred.

God had entered the world as a baby.

God Came Near

*H*e's been to Bethlehem, wearing barn rags and hearing sheep crunch. Suckling milk and shivering against the cold. All of divinity content to cocoon itself in an eight-pound body and to sleep on a cow's supper. Millions who face the chill of empty pockets or the fears of sudden change turn to Christ. Why?

Because he's been there.

3:16: Numbers of Hope

Jacob's Gift

$\mathcal{S}$uppose you could give Jesus a gift this Christmas. My, what an opportunity. You'd hold nothing back. Spare no expense. Withhold no effort. Wouldn't you give him your finest offering? What if you had the chance to carry a gift to the throne of Christ?

You do.

When you love his children, you love him. "Whatever you did for one of the least of these brothers and sisters of mine, you did for me" (Matt. 25:40 NIV). Would you like to give Jesus a Christmas gift? Then love one of his needy children.

This was the discovery of the main character in the next story. May it be your discovery too.

*R*abbi Simeon brushed sawdust off his hands. "I have a special announcement." All but one apprentice in the shop stopped to listen.

"Jacob," the rabbi instructed, "our work is finished for the day." Jacob didn't respond.

Jacob only heard the *swish–swish* of the saw. The other boys in the shop began to snicker.

Rabbi Simeon let out a deep sigh and shook his head, but down deep he was pleased. He knew what it was like to get lost in the world of woodworking. But it was time to go home.

"Jacob!" the rabbi called again.

The sawing stopped. "I'm sorry, Rabbi," Jacob said softly.

Rabbi Simeon smiled. "It's all right. Put away your tools and hang up your apron."

Jacob hung up his apron as the other boys continued to snicker. Finally the rabbi spoke, and all eyes turned to him.

"My nephew from Nazareth should be here in a few days. He is a master carpenter who will help me select one of you for a special task. The one who builds the best project will work with me on the new synagogue."

I just have to be chosen, Jacob determined. I want to use my hands to help build God's house.

The rabbi was speaking. "I'll be away for the next three days, but you may all use the workshop to finish your projects." As the others began to leave, the rabbi asked Jacob to stay.

Jacob waited till everyone had left and then approached the carpenter. "I'm sorry, Rabbi," he apologized. "I'll do better next time."

The rabbi motioned for Jacob to sit on one of the stools. "Jacob, you've done nothing wrong. I need to tell you something." The rabbi smiled and continued. "God has given you the gift of woodworking. What is difficult for many is easy for you. Surely, you've noticed."

Jacob nodded. He had wondered why other boys struggled to make things that seemed so simple to him.

"God gives gifts, Jacob. You have a special gift. Have you ever wondered why God gave you the gift of woodworking?"

"So I can learn to be a good carpenter?"

"Well." The rabbi chuckled. "Not exactly. God gave you this gift to share with others. Let's say you gave a present to one of my daughters. How do you think that would make me feel?"

"Happy?"

"Of course. Even though you gave the gift to my child, I would feel like you had given it to me. God is like that too. So when we give a gift to one of God's children, it's like giving a gift to him."

"Now, run home and tell your father that I hope he has an inn full of guests next week."

"We're expecting a lot of business, son," Jacob's father reminded him that evening.

"I will work on my project in the mornings," Jacob promised, "and help you in the evenings."

The next three mornings Jacob worked hard to complete his project. He was building a new kind of animal feed trough with wheels.

On the night before Rabbi Simeon returned, Jacob went to the workshop after helping his father at the inn. Jacob looked at his project. *I must finish tonight*, he thought. *So much work still to do. But I'm so tired. Maybe if I close my eyes for a few minutes . . .*

The next moment, a beam of starlight slipped through a crack and fell across Jacob's napping eyes. "What!" he shouted, startled by the sudden light. Had he slept through the night? Then he looked out and saw a gleaming, shimmering light in the night.

Jacob rubbed the sleep from his eyes as he walked outside and toward the star that seemed to dance in the sky over the stable behind his father's inn.

As he got closer, he heard a strange sound. He looked through a hole in the stable wall.

A baby was in a tiny nest of straw on the ground!

Beside the baby knelt his mother and a man. The baby must be uncomfortable on the ground, Jacob thought.

Jacob raced back to the workshop. He stood beside his feed trough. Tomorrow the rabbi would select the best project.

But tonight there's a new baby without a place to sleep . . .

❧

"Good morning, boys," said Rabbi Simeon.

Jacob approached the rabbi. "Uh, sir . . . I need to tell you something."

"Later, Jacob. We need to get everything ready. Where is your project?"

"Uh . . . something happened. A big star—"

"Uncle Simeon!" said a man at the door.

"Joseph!" Simeon shouted. "I'm so glad you're here!"

Jacob's eyes widened. This was the man he had seen with the baby in the stable the night before.

"Jacob, this is my nephew from Nazareth."

"We've already met," said Joseph. "In fact, Jacob gave my newborn son his very first gift."

"Your son?" the rabbi inquired. "Where is he?'

"Come, and I'll show you."

Joseph led the rabbi and Jacob past the inn toward a shelter. "The stable?" Simeon asked. "You kept your baby in a—"

Joseph smiled. "Shh, Uncle. They're asleep."

When the rabbi looked inside, he saw a beautiful newborn baby.

"His name is Jesus," Joseph whispered. "And his cradle is fit for a king."

Joseph's kindness made Jacob's cheeks turn red.

"Tell me, Jacob," said the rabbi, "why did you decide to give your feed trough away?"

"I remembered what you said. 'When you give a gift to one of God's children, you give a gift to God.'"

The rabbi's voice was soft. "And so you have, my son. So you have."

*J*oseph. The quiet father of Jesus. Rather than make a name for himself, he made a home for Christ. And because he did, a great reward came his way. "He called His name Jesus" (Matt. 1:25 NKJV).

Queue up the millions who have spoken the name of Jesus, and look at the person selected to stand at the front of the line. Joseph. Of all the saints, sinners, prodigals, and preachers who have spoken the name, Joseph, a blue-collar, small-town construction worker said it first. He cradled the wrinkle-faced prince of heaven, and with an audience of angels and pigs, whispered, "Jesus . . . You'll be called Jesus."

Seems right, don't you think? Joseph gave up his name. So Jesus let Joseph say his.

CURE FOR THE COMMON LIFE

An Angel's
Story

There has been born for you a Savior, who is Christ the Lord" (Luke 2:11 NASB). The Greek word used in this verse is *Kyrios*. It signifies one who rightfully holds a position of authority. Jesus was born with this title. He has lawful right to rule over every star, sphere, galaxy, and gulf. He is lord of legislators, liberators, light bearers, and laborers. He bears the signet of the highest office and wears the insignia of:

"Lord of all" (Acts 10:36 NIV).

"Lord of both the dead and the living" (Rom. 14:9 NIV).

"Head over every . . . authority" (Col. 2:10 NIV).

For Christmas, God gave you the perfect gift. A Lord to lead you. Congress doesn't run the world; the Lord Jesus does. The economy doesn't determine your future; the Lord Jesus does. Cancer doesn't control your destiny, death doesn't have the last word, the faceless hand of fate isn't directing history. The Lord Jesus is.

You have a Lord to lead you.

Another Greek word for *Lord* is *despotes*, from which we draw the unfavorable English word *despot*. A despot is a pretender and usurper. Satan fits this qualification. Had he had his way, Jesus the Lord would have never entered Mary's womb.

Spiritual beings populate the stories of Scripture. Angels singing. Demons infecting. Heavenly hosts fighting. Satan's gremlins invading. Ignore the armies of God and Satan and you ignore the heart of Scripture. Ever since the snake tempted Eve in Eden, we've known: there is more to this world than meets the eye.

We know less than we desire about these beings.

Their appearance? Their number? Their strategies and plans? We can only imagine.

Several years ago, stirred by an article by David Lambert, I envisioned the Christmas conflict between the true Lord and his challenger. Surely there was much. If Satan could preempt Christ in the cradle, there'd be no Christ on the cross. Don't you think he tried?

The conflict was, no doubt, far grander and more dramatic than anything we can fictionalize. But while we can only imagine if such a war occurred, we don't have to wonder who would win it. We can be sure of this: we know who won. Because we know he came.

$\mathcal{G}$abriel."

Just the sound of my King's voice stirred my heart. I left my post at the entryway and stepped into the throne room. To my left was the desk on which sat the Book of Life. Ahead of me was the throne of Almighty God. I entered the circle of unceasing light, folded my wings before me to cover my face, and knelt before him. "Yes, my Lord?"

"You have served the kingdom well. You are a noble messenger. Never have you flinched in duty. Never have you flagged in zeal."

I bowed my head, basking in the words. "Whatever you ask, I'll do a thousand times over, my King," I promised.

"Of that I have no doubt, dear messenger." His voice assumed a solemnity I'd never heard him use. "But your greatest work lies ahead of you. Your next assignment is to carry a gift to Earth. Behold."

I lifted my eyes to see a necklace—a clear vial on a golden chain—dangling from his extended hand.

My Father spoke earnestly, "Though empty, this vial will soon contain my greatest gift. Place it around your neck."

I was about to take it when a raspy voice interrupted me. "And what treasure will you send to Earth this time?"

My back stiffened at the irreverent tone, and my stomach turned at the sudden stench. Such foul odor could come from only one being. I drew my sword and turned to do battle with Lucifer.

The Father's hand on my shoulder stopped me.

"Worry not, Gabriel. He will do no harm."

I stepped back and stared at God's enemy. He was completely covered. A black cassock hung over his skeletal frame, hiding his body and arms and hooding his face. The feet, protruding beneath the robe, were thrice-toed and clawed. The skin on his hands was that of a snake. Talons extended from his fingers. He pulled his cape farther over his face as a shield against the light, but the brightness still pained him. Seeking relief, he turned toward me. I caught a glimpse of a skullish face within the cowl.

"What are you staring at, Gabriel?" he sneered. "Are you that glad to see me?"

I had no words for this fallen angel. Both what I saw and what I remembered left me speechless. I remembered him before the rebellion: poised proudly at the vanguard of our force, wings wide, holding forth a radiant sword; he had inspired us to do the same. Who could refuse him? The sight of his velvet hair and coal-black eyes had far outstripped the beauty of any celestial being.

Any being, of course, except our Creator. No one compared Lucifer to God . . . except Lucifer. How he came to think he was worthy of the same worship as God, only God knows. All I knew was that I had not seen Satan since the rebellion. And what I now saw repulsed me.

I searched for just a hint of his former splendor but saw none.

"Your news must be urgent," spat Satan to God, still unable to bear the light.

My Father's response was a pronouncement. "The time has come for the second gift."

The frame beneath the cape bounced stiffly as Lucifer chuckled. "The second gift, eh? I hope it works better than the first."

"You're disappointed with the first?" asked the Father.

"Oh, quite the contrary; I've delighted in it." Lifting a bony finger, he spelled a word in the air:

C-H-O-I-C-E.

"You gave Adam his choice," Satan scoffed. "And what a choice he made! He chose me. Ever since the fruit was plucked from the tree in the Garden, I've held your children captive. They fell. Fast. Hard. They are mine. You have failed. Heh-heh-heh."

"You speak so confidently," replied the Father, astounding me with his patience.

Lucifer stepped forward, his cloak dragging behind him. "Of course! I thwart everything you do! You soften hearts, I harden them. You teach truth, I shadow it. You offer joy, I steal it."

He pivoted and paraded around the room, boasting of his deeds. "The betrayal of Joseph by his brothers—I did that. Moses banished to the desert after killing the Egyptian—I did that. David watching Bathsheba bathe— that was me. You must admit my work has been crafty."

"Crafty? Perhaps. But effective? No. I know what you will do even before you do it. I used the betrayal of Joseph to deliver my people from famine. Your banishment of Moses became his wilderness training. And yes, David did commit adultery with Bathsheba—but he repented of his sin! And thousands have been inspired by his example and found what he found—unending grace. Your deceptions have only served as platforms for my mercy. You are still my servant, Satan. When will you learn? Your feeble attempts to disturb my work only enable my work. Every act you have intended for evil, I have used for good."

Satan began to growl—a throaty, guttural, angry growl. Softly at first, then louder, until the room was filled with a roar that must have quaked the foundations of hell.

But the King was not bothered. "Feeling ill?"

Lucifer lurked around the room, breathing loudly, searching for words to say and a shadow from which to say them. He finally found the words but never the shadow. "Show me, O King of light, show me one person on Earth who always does right and obeys your will."

"Dare you ask? You know there need be only one perfect one, only one sinless one to die for all the others."

"I know your plans—and you have *failed*! No Messiah will come from your people. There is none who is sinless. Not one." He turned his back to the desk and began naming the children. "Not Moses. Not Abraham. Not Lot. Not Rebekah. Not Elijah . . ."

The Father stood up from his throne, releasing a wave of holy light so intense that Lucifer staggered backward and fell.

"Those are my children you mock," God's voice boomed. "You think you know much, fallen angel, but you know little. Your mind dwells in the valley of self. Your eyes see no further than your needs."

The King walked over and reached for the book. He turned it toward Lucifer and commanded, "Come, Deceiver, read the name of the One who will call your bluff. Read the name of the One who will storm your gates."

Satan rose slowly off his haunches. Like a wary wolf, he walked a wide circle toward the desk until he stood before the volume and read the word:

"Immanuel?" he muttered to himself, then spoke in a tone of disbelief. "God with us?"

For the first time the hooded head turned squarely toward the face of the Father. "No. Not even you would do that. Not even you would go so far."

"You've never believed me, Satan."

"But *Immanuel*? The plan is bizarre! You don't know what it is like on Earth! You don't know how dark I've made it. It's putrid. It's evil. It's . . ."

"It is mine," proclaimed the King. "And I will reclaim what is mine. I will become flesh. I will feel what my creatures feel. I will see what they see."

"But what of their sin?"

"I will bring mercy."

"What of their death?"

"I will give life."

Satan stood speechless.

God spoke, "I love my children. Love does not take away the beloved's freedom. But love takes away fear. And Immanuel will leave behind a tribe of fearless children. They will not fear you or your hell."

Satan stepped back at the thought. His retort was childish. "Th-th-they will too!"

"I will take away all sin. I will take away death. Without sin and without death, you have no power."

Around and around in a circle Satan paced, clenching and unclenching his wiry fingers. When he finally stopped, he asked a question that even I was thinking. "Why? Why would you do this?"

The Father's voice was deep and soft. "Because I love them."

The two stood facing each other. Neither spoke. The extremes of the universe were before me. God robed in light, each thread glowing. Satan canopied in evil, the very fabric of his robe seeming to crawl. Peace contrasting panic. Wisdom confronting foolishness. One able to rescue, the other anxious to condemn.

I have reflected much on what happened next. Though I have relived the moment countless times, I'm as stunned as I was at the first. Never in my wildest thoughts did I think my King would do what he did. Had he demanded Satan's departure, who would have questioned? Had he taken Satan's life, who would have grieved? Had he called me to attack, I would have been willing. But God did none of these.

From the circle of light came his extended hand.

From his throne came an honest invitation. "Will you surrender? Will you return to me?"

I do not know the thoughts of Satan. But I believe that for a fleeting second the evil heart softened. The head cocked slightly, as if amazed that such an offer would be made. But then it yanked itself erect.

"Where will we battle?" he challenged.

The Father sighed at the dark angel's resistance. "On a hill called Calvary."

"If you make it that far." Satan smirked, spinning and marching out the entryway. I watched as his spiny wings extended, and he soared into the heavenlies.

The Father stood motionless for a moment, then turned back to the book. Opening to the final chapter, He slowly read words I had never heard. No sentences. Just words. Saying each, then pausing:

Jesus,
Nail,
Cross,
Blood,
Tomb,
Life.

He motioned toward me, and I responded, kneeling again before him. Handing me the necklace, he explained, "This vial will contain the essence of myself; a seed to be placed in the womb of a young girl. Her name is Mary. She lives among my chosen people. The fruit of the seed is the Son of God. Take it to her."

"But how will I know her?" I asked.

"Don't worry. You will."

I could not comprehend God's plan, but my understanding was not essential. My obedience was. I lowered my head, and he draped the chain around my neck. Amazingly, the vial was no longer empty. It glowed with light.

"Jesus. Tell her to call my Son *Jesus*."

How thrilling had been our send-off! Michael, the archangel, read to us the words from the Book of Courage. The troops sang to the Father, begging his Spirit to accompany our battalion. The Father rose from his throne in a flood of cascading light and gave us words of strength.

To the angels he urged, "Be strong, my ministers."

To me he reminded, "Gabriel, Satan desires to destroy the seed as much as you desire to deliver it. But fear not. I am with you."

"Thy will be done," I resolved and took my place at the apex of the troops. It was time to leave. I began the song of praise to signal our departure. One by one the angels joined me in worship and sang. One final time I faced the light. We turned and plunged into the heavenlies.

On the wave of his light we flew. On the crest of our songs we soared. Paragon was at my right, Aegus on my left. Both handpicked by our Father to guard the vial. Ever able. Ever nimble. Ever obedient.

So immense was our number that I could not see its end. Our strength knew no bounds. We flew as a torrent of stars through the universe: I at the helm, thousands of angels behind me. I delighted in a backward glance at the flood of silver wings rising and falling in silent rhythm.

From them came a constant flow of spontaneous praise.

"To God be all glory!"

"Only he is worthy!"

"Mighty is the King of kings and Lord of lords!"

"The battle belongs to God!"

I had chosen only the most able angels for my

company, for only the most able could face the foe. Every angel had been willing, but only the most skilled warriors had been chosen.

We passed the galaxy of Ebon into the constellation of Emmanees. Out of the corner of my eye I caught a glimpse of Exalon, a planet ringed once for every child found faithful to the Father. Through the constellation of Clarion and into the stellar circle of Darius.

Around my neck dangled the glowing vial, its mystery still beyond my understanding.

Behind me I heard the soft voice of Sophio. The Father has gifted him with wisdom, and I have taken him on many journeys. His task is always the same. "Whisper truth to me as we fly," I tell him, and so he does. "Lucifer is the father of lies. There is no truth . . . no truth in him. He comes to steal, kill, and destroy."

As my courage mounted, so did my speed. We knew we would not fail. But we had no idea that the battle would come so soon. Only moments across the ridge of time, Paragon shouted, "Prepare yourselves!"

Suddenly I was entangled in an invisible net. Row after row of angels tumbled in upon me. Even the final flank was moving too fast to avoid the trap. Within moments, we were a ball of confusion: wings flapping against wings. Angels bumping into angels.

Before we could draw our swords, our attackers drew the net so tight we couldn't move. From within the fray I could hear them mocking us.

"*You're* the best of heaven? Ha!"

"To the pit with you!"

"Now you will face the true master!" they taunted.

But their celebration was premature. The King had prepared me for this web of evil. I knew exactly what to do.

"Holy, holy, holy is the Lord God Almighty!" I shouted.

"Holy, holy, holy is the Lord God Almighty!" Over and over I praised my Master. My angels heard me and joined the worship.

Weakened by the words of truth, the hellhounds released the ropes, allowing us to break free.

"The Lord loves those who praise him!" Sophio shouted in triumph.

Liberated, we brandished our swords of light, each connecting with the next, forming a seamless ball of brilliance. Blinded, the demons crashed into each other and then scrambled to escape. I dispatched a platoon to pursue them. "Make sure they don't return!" I instructed.

I studied our flanks—first one side, then the other. No losses. The attack had only increased our resolve. I began to sing, and we resumed our journey, bathed in the Light of our swords and the music of our adoration.

We passed the golden planet, Escholada, signifying our entrance into the chosen galaxy. Each of us knows well these stars. We frequent them on missions. Despite our fond memories of these constellations, we did not pause. Our mission was too vital.

"Gabriel." It was Paragon calling my name. "Behold, in the distance."

I had never seen such a demon. His jackal-like head sat on a long, scaly neck and dragon body. His wings stretched so wide they could engulf a dozen of my fighters. Each of his four feet appeared strong enough to crush an angel. "Who is he?" I asked Paragon and Aegus. It was Sophio who answered.

"It is Phlumar."

"Phlumar? It couldn't be!" Before the rebellion he was our chief singer and most noble fighter. He would often fly ahead of us, suspended on the graceful rising and falling of lustrous wings. Many of the songs I now sing, I'd first heard from the lips of Phlumar. *Now look at him*, I thought.

What happened to the sterling eyes and white robe? What happened to the countenance of joy? As I drew near, the repugnant smell of evil caused me to wince. I readied my sword, expecting an attack. I did not expect a question.

"My friend, how long has it been?" The voice was as warm as an archdemon can feign.

"Not long enough, child of hell," I shouted in his face as I soared past. I didn't trust myself to stop. I didn't trust my emotions or my strength. I kept moving, but immediately he was next to me.

"Gabriel, you must listen to me."

"Your prince is a liar and the father of lies."

"But my prince has changed," Phlumar argued.

I did not slow down. Out of the corner of my eye I saw Aegus and Paragon flying wide-eyed with their hands on their swords, awaiting my command. I prayed that they wouldn't see the concern in my eyes. If Phlumar had retained one-tenth of his strength, he could destroy an entire battalion before I could respond. He had been the mightiest in our class.

Phlumar continued, "A miracle has occurred since you left on your mission. My master witnessed your utter defeat of our forces. He is disturbed by your strength and his weakness. He is equally perplexed by the offer of mercy which came in the throne room. He says you were there, Gabriel. Did you see it?"

Though I didn't respond, the image of God's extended hand came to mind. I thought of the tilted head and remembered my first impressions. Could it be that Satan's heart indeed had softened?

Emotion accompanied Phlumar's plea. "Come, Gabriel. Talk with Prince Lucifer. Plead with him on the Father's behalf. Speak of your Master's love. He will listen to you. Let us go together and urge him to repent."

Phlumar accelerated ahead of me and stopped, forcing me to do the same. He towered above me. I thought I'd prepared for everything, but this I never expected. I prayed for direction.

"Together, Gabriel, you and I together again," the dragon continued. "It can happen. We can be united. Satan's heart is ripe; already mine is changed."

Suddenly it hit me. Again, I knew what to do. I silently thanked God for his guidance.

"Your heart has changed, has it, Phlumar?"

His huge head nodded up and down. I turned to Paragon and Aegus. The fear on their faces was giving way to curiosity.

"You long to join our ranks, do you?"

"Yes, Gabriel, I do. The rebellion was a mistake. Come with me. We will reason with Lucifer. I long to return to heaven. I long to know my former splendor."

By now my plan was clear. "Wonderful news, Phlumar!"

I sensed the surprise on the faces of my angels. "Our God is a good God," I announced. "Slow to anger and quick to forgive. Surely he has heard your confession." I paused and elevated closer to his face and looked into his eyes. "Let us then lift our voices together in praise."

Fear flashed across Phlumar's face. Sophio, perceiving my strategy, announced the truth: "You must worship the Lord your God!"

"But—but—but I don't remember any of the words."

Realizing Phlumar's true intent, my soldiers began to encircle him. I moved even closer and spoke firmly,

"Surely you are willing to worship our Master. Surely you haven't forgotten the songs of worship. Open your mouth and confess the name of the Lord!"

Phlumar looked to the right and left but saw no escape. "Join us," I dared. "If your heart is truly changed, worship with us." I pulled out my sword. "If not, prepare to fight us."

Phlumar knew he'd been foiled. His mouth would not—*could not*—praise the Almighty God. His heart belonged to Satan. He swung his neck to one side, preparing to sweep us into the next galaxy. Had we only *our* strength he would have succeeded. The collective might of our troops could not have resisted his force. But we were empowered from on high. And endued with God's strength, we pounced on the demon in a second.

Before he had a chance to attack, his leathery skin was invaded by swords of light. It melted like wax. What little flesh still clung to his bones was instantly blotched and infected. Froth fell from his jaws. He opened his mouth and howled a cry as lonely as the skies have heard.

"Kill me," he begged, his voice now husky. He knew any death we gave him would be gracious in comparison to the punishment which awaited him from the hands of Lucifer.

"The angels are kept in bonds for judgment," I reminded him. "Only the Father can kill the eternal." With a twist of our swords we cast this demon of death into the abyss. For an instant I was sorrowful for this creature. But the sorrow was brief as I remembered how quickly he had followed the prince and his false promises.

I lifted my voice in praise both for our victory and my salvation. I could not help but think of the prophecy the Father spoke to me: "As much as we seek to bring the seed, so Satan seeks to destroy it."

Lifting hands heavenward, we proclaimed his name above all names as we resumed our journey. Soon we came into the Earth's solar system. I lifted my head as a signal for the army to slow down. The atmosphere of Terra surrounded us, and I searched for the tiny strip of land inhabited by the promised people.

How precious is this globe to him! I thought. Other orbs are larger. Others grander. But none so suited for Adam and his children. And now the hour of the delivery was at hand. Below me was the small town where God's chosen one slept.

"I see you have made it safely."

It was the voice I dreaded. Instantly he was before us. We had no option but to stop.

"You are wearing your old uniform, Lucifer," I accused.

The true angels were entranced at his appearance. As was I. Was this the same devil who had repulsed me in the throne room?

His hoarse whisper was now a vibrant baritone. The skeletal figure now robust and statuesque. Next to his light, our whiteness was gray and dirty. Next to his voice, our voices were but a whimper. We raised our swords, but they flickered like candles against the sun.

My battalions looked upon the devil in confusion. Before the send-off Michael had tried to warn them, but no words prepare you for Lucifer. Without speaking a word, he enchants. Without lifting a weapon, he disarms. Without a touch, he seduces. Angels have been known to follow him without resistance.

But I had the words of the Father in my heart. "He has been a liar since the beginning."

The devil looked at me with a soft smile. "Gabriel, Gabriel. How many times have I spoken your name? My servants can tell you. I have followed you through the years. You are one loyal angel. And now your loyalty is rewarded. The mission of missions."

He threw back his head and laughed, not an evil laugh but a godlike one. *How well he imitates the King!*

"It's no imitation," he said as if he could read my mind. "It's genuine. I rejoice that you have passed our test."

My face betrayed my perplexity.

"Has he not informed you, my friend? How wise is our heavenly Father. How gracious that he should allow me the privilege of telling you. This has been a trial of your loyalty. Your whole mission was a test. The Day of Sorrows. The heavenly rebellion. The falling of the angels. My visit in the throne room. The net. Phlumar. All of that was to test you, to train you. And now, O Gabriel, the King and I congratulate you. You have proven faithful."

I thought I knew every scheme of Lucifer, every misdeed, every lie. I thought I had anticipated each possible move. I was wrong. This one I never imagined . . . Oh, is he sly. He sounded so sincere.

"Do you honestly think I could rebel against God?" he implored. "The Father of Truth? Why, I love him."

His grand voice choked with emotion. "He created me. He gave me free will. And all this time I have worshiped him from afar so that you could be tested. And now, my friend, you have passed the Father's test. Why else would he allow you to witness my visit to heaven? It was all a staged event: God's magnum opus to test your dedication."

His words tugged at my breast. My sword dropped to one side and my shield to the other. My thoughts swam. *What is this I feel? What is this power? I know he is evil, yet I find myself weakening. I, at once, long to love and kill him, to trust and deny him.* I turned to look at Aegus and Paragon. They, too, had dropped their weapons, their faces softening as they began to believe the words the Deceiver spoke. Behind them, our armies were relaxing. One by one the swords were dimming. Incredible. With only a few words Lucifer could harness legions. *Is this really true? He looks and sounds so much like the Father* . . . All of us were beginning to fall under his control.

All, that is, except one. In the distance I saw Sophio.

His eyes were not on Lucifer. He was looking heavenward. I could hear his declaration, mounting in volume with each phrase. "Neither death nor life, neither angels nor demons, neither the present nor the future, nor any powers, neither height nor depth, nor anything else in all creation, will be able to separate us from the love of God!"

Sophio's prayer was a beam into the sky. With my eyes I followed the shaft of light. At its end I could see my Father standing. One glimpse of his glory and my confusion cleared. I snapped erect and repositioned my shield. Lucifer, for the first time, saw Sophio praying. His smile vanished; then he forced it to return.

He spoke faster, but the true rasp of his voice was returning. "The Father awaits us, Gabriel. Let us smash the vial in celebration of the Father's victory. Let us return with joy. Your mission is complete. You will be rewarded with a throne like mine. You will be like God."

If Satan had any chance, he just lost it. "Liar!" I defied. "I have heard those words before. I have heard that promise. It is a lie, and you are the father of lies. You stink, you buzzard. To hell with you!"

Though I knew my sword would not stop Lucifer,

still I unsheathed my weapon. "Almighty God, save us!" I prayed. He did. My sword projected a light far greater than ever before—a light so bright that Lucifer covered his eyes and released a deluge of curses.

I turned to my angels; they were again alert and poised, the spell broken and their courage restored. They lifted their swords in defiance. The ever-increasing light illuminated the devil, revealing what I had seen in the throne room, only now his hood lay back. The skullish face violated the sky.

I drove my light into the devil's heart. As I did, Aegus did the same from the other side.

Satan screamed, writhing in pain as our lights fused in purging heat. From within him scampered the ogres of a thousand miseries: loneliness, anger, fear.

In one final, desperate attempt, Lucifer twisted toward me and lunged at heaven's vial.

He never had a chance. Paragon's sword swept out of the sky, severing Satan's hand from his arm, sending it spiraling into the night. A wave of stench forced us to lift our shields before our faces. Satan threw back his head, his visage contorted in pain. The voice which only moments before had charmed, now hissed.

"I'll be back!" Lucifer swore. "I'll be back."

Sophio shook his head in disgust. "Disguised as an angel of light . . . ," he said softly.

As quickly as he had appeared, Satan was gone. And we erupted in praise.

"Holy, holy, holy is the Lord God Almighty!"

"King of kings and Lord of lords!"

As the Father received our praise, he whispered to me. I heard him as if at my side. "Go, Gabriel, go and tell Mary."

On a wave of worship I flew, this time alone. I circled through the clouds and over the ground. Below me was the city where Mary was born. The Father was right; I knew her in an instant. Her heart had no shadow. Her soul was as pure as any I've seen.

I made the final descent. "Mary." I kept my voice low so as not to startle her.

She turned but saw nothing. Then I realized I was invisible to her. I waved my wings before my body and incarnated. She covered her face at the light and shrank into the protection of the doorway.

"Don't be afraid," I urged.

The minute I spoke, she looked up toward the sky.

Again I was amazed. I praised my Father for his wisdom. Her heart is so flawless, so willing. "Greetings. God be with you."

Her eyes widened, and she turned as if to run. "Mary, you have nothing to fear. You have found favor with God. You will become pregnant and give birth to a son and call his name Jesus. He will be great. He will be called the Son of the Highest. The Lord God will give him the throne of his father David; he will rule Jacob's house forever—no end, ever, to his kingdom."

Though she was listening, she was puzzled.

"But how? I've never slept with a man."

Before I spoke I looked up into the heavens. The Father was standing, giving me his blessing.

I continued, "The Holy Spirit will come upon you, the power of the Highest hover over you; therefore, the child you bring to birth will be called holy, Son of God. Nothing, you see, is impossible with God."

Mary looked at me, then up into the sky. For a long time she gazed into the blueness, so long that I, too, looked up. Did she see the angels? Did the heavens open? I do not know. But I do know when I looked back at her, she was smiling.

"Yes, I see it all now: I'm the Lord's maid, ready to serve. Let it be with me just as you say."

As she spoke, a light appeared in her womb. I glanced at the vial. It was empty.

Joseph led the donkey off the side of the road and rubbed his hand over his forehead. "Let's find a place to spend the night. It'll be dark before we reach Bethlehem."

Mary didn't respond. Joseph walked around the side of the animal and looked into his wife's face. She was asleep! Chin on her chest, hands on her stomach. How had she been able to doze off while riding on the back of a donkey?

Suddenly her head popped up and her eyes opened. "Are we there?"

"No." The young husband smiled. "We still have several hours to go. I see an inn up ahead. Shall we spend the night?"

"Oh, Joseph. I'm feeling we should continue until we reach Bethlehem." Then she paused. "Perhaps we can stop for a rest."

He sighed, smiled, squeezed her hand, and resumed his place, leading the donkey toward the simple structure on the side of the road. "It's crowded," Joseph said as he lowered Mary to the ground. It took several minutes for Joseph to find a bench where the two could sit.

"I'll return in a moment with something to eat."

Joseph elbowed his way through the crowd. He turned around in time to see a woman take his empty seat next to Mary. Mary started to object, but then she smiled, looked through the crowd at Joseph, and shrugged.

Not an unkind bone in her body, he mused.

Of all the bizarre events over the last few months, he was sure of one thing: the heart of his wife. He'd never met anyone like her. Her story that an angel appeared in the middle of the afternoon? Could have been some kid playing a trick. His memory of an angel appearing in his sleep? Could have been from God . . . could have been from too much wine. Her story about her uncle being struck speechless until the cousin was born? Could have been laryngitis.

But her story about being a pregnant virgin? Mary doesn't lie. She's as pure as an angel. So if Mary says she's a virgin, she is. If she says the baby is the Son of God, let's just hope he gets his nose from the Father's side of the family.

Mary—round-faced and short—wasn't a beauty by any means. A bit hefty even before she was pregnant. But her eyes always twinkled, and her heart was bigger than the Mediterranean. She had an ever-present smile and the countenance of a person about to deliver the punch line of a good joke. That's what made Mary, Mary. Joseph shook his head as Mary pushed herself to her feet so the husband of the woman who'd taken Joseph's seat could sit down.

The man started to object, but she waved him off. "I need to stand for a minute," she mouthed to Joseph as she walked in his direction. Or waddled in his direction. They'd both hoped the baby would come in Nazareth; at least they had family there. They knew no one in Bethlehem.

Joseph tucked her arm in his, and the two leaned against a wall. "You sure you want to go farther?"

She nodded, and after more than a few "excuse me"s and "pardon me"s, the two found their way to the door.

"One more drink of water?" Mary asked.

"Of course. Wait outside."

Mary leaned against a tree as Joseph stood in line at the well. She smiled at the way he quickly struck up a conversation with the man in front of him. When he returned carrying water, the man came with him.

"Mary, this is Simon. He's also going to Bethlehem and has offered us a place to sit in his ox cart."

"That's kind of you."

Simon smiled. "I'd enjoy the company. Just tie your donkey to the back."

"Excuse me. I heard you say Bethlehem. Would you have room for one more?"

The request came from an old man with a long silver beard and the fringes of a rabbi. Simon quickly nodded.

After helping Mary into the wagon, Joseph turned to help the rabbi. "What was your name?"

"Gabriel," I answered and took a seat across from Mary.

Aegus hovered in front of the wagon and Paragon behind. Both were alert, wings spread and swords drawn. Up until the stop at the inn, I had flown with them. But something seemed suspicious about the wagon, so I took the form of a person. I quickly regretted not having chosen the appearance of a young merchant (the beard I wore itched horribly).

My battalion didn't need me to remind them, but I did anyway: "Hell does not want Immanuel born. Stay alert."

Invisible angels a dozen deep encircled the wagon. I smiled to myself. Simon could have driven blindfolded. There was no way this cart would have failed to reach its destination.

The congested road slowed our progress. We traveled no faster than those around us on foot, but at least Mary could rest. She closed her eyes and leaned her head against the side of the wagon. I could see the radiance in her womb. He glowed like a healing fire. I worshiped him, even unborn. My heart celebrated with silent songs of praise which he could hear. I smiled as Mary felt him move. Around me the army heard my song and joined in praise.

About an hour later I sensed it. Evil. My body tensed. The feel of deviltry was on the road, lurking among the travelers. I alerted the angels. "Be ready." Sophio entered the cart and whispered, "He prowls as a lion, looking for someone to devour." I nodded in agreement and searched the faces of those walking near the wagon.

A young man approached the cart. He asked Mary, "You look tired. Would you like some water?" Mary said, "Thank you," and reached for the offered wineskin. I jumped to my feet, purposefully bumping the demon's arm. The water pouch fell to the ground as Mary and Joseph heard me apologize. Only the young man heard me challenge him: "Beast of hell, you shall not touch this daughter of God."

The demon vacated the body of the man and drew a sword. "You have no chance this time, Gabriel," he cried, and suddenly dozens of demons appeared from all sides and raced toward Mary.

"Joseph," she spoke, her face full of pain as she held her womb, "something's wrong. It—it's like something's hitting me in the stomach. I'm in terrible pain."

Instantly I assumed angelic form and wrapped myself around her as a shield. The demons' swords pierced me. I felt their sting—but she was safe. Just then Paragon and seven angels appeared, slashing at the demons' backs. The demons were distracted but determined.

The wagon began to shake. Travelers began to panic.

I heard a cry. I looked up in time to see Simon clutch his throat. His face was red, and his eyes bulged. Around his neck I could see the spiny fingers of a troll. Another demon had bewitched the ox, causing it to lurch spastically toward the side of the road.

Someone screamed, "Stop the wagon; there's a cliff ahead!"

A courageous man attempted to grab the reins, but he couldn't move. Afterward he told people he was frozen with fear. I knew otherwise: a demon had webbed him to the road.

Simon gasped for breath and slumped sideways on the seat. I knew he was dead. The possessed animal swerved madly toward the cliff. I looked at Mary. Joseph's arm was around her shoulders; her hand was on her round stomach. I knew that in a matter of seconds we would crash over the edge into the valley below. The driver was dead; the wagon was out of control. I turned and prayed to the only One who could help.

From the womb, he spoke. His parents did not hear. The word was not for the ears of Mary and Joseph. Only the hosts of heaven and hell could hear the word. And when they did, all stopped. "Life!"

The command flooded the wagon as totally as it had flooded Eden. The demons began scattering like rats.

"Life!" came the command a second time. Simon coughed as air filled his lungs. "The reins!" I shouted. He gasped, grabbed the reins, and pulled himself erect. Through watery eyes he saw the edge of the road and instinctively yanked the animal back until it stopped. We were safe.

But even with the demons gone, I took no chances. My command to Sophio was urgent. "They found her on the road; they will find her room at the inn. Do what needs to be done." Sophio saluted and soared ahead to the inn at Bethlehem.

Mary remained enveloped in my light. Joseph watched her with alarm; she relaxed in my care. "I'm better now," she said. "What happened to the rabbi?"

*

"But don't you have just one room?" Joseph pleaded.

"To be honest, I did. But only moments ago a large delegation arrived and took every last bed. I don't have a place for you and your wife."

Joseph tried to be patient, but his jaw was tightening.

He leaned forward so his face was inches from the inn-keeper's. "See that lady in the cart?" he asked through his teeth. "She is my wife. She could deliver any minute. She nearly had the baby this afternoon in a wagon. She is in pain right now. Do you want the baby to be born here in your doorway?"

"No, of course not, but I can't help you. Please understand. I have no more rooms."

"I heard you, but it is midnight and cold. Don't you have any place for us to keep warm?"

The man sighed, looked at Mary and then at Joseph. He walked into his house and returned with a lamp. "Behind the inn is a trail that will lead you down a hill. Follow it until you come to a stable. It's clean, at least as clean as stables usually are." With a shrug he added, "You'll be warm there."

Joseph couldn't believe what he was hearing. "You expect us to stay in the stable?"

"Joseph." It was Mary speaking. She'd heard every word. He turned; she was smiling. He knew exactly what the smile meant. Enough arguing.

His sigh puffed his cheeks. "That will be fine," Joseph consented and took the lamp.

"Strange," the clerk muttered to himself as the couple left. Turning to his wife he asked, "Who was the man who took all the rooms?"

Opening the register, the woman read the name aloud. "Different name. Sophio. Must be Greek."

We were a wreath of light around the stable, a necklace of diamonds around the structure. Every angel had been called from his post for the coming, even Michael. None doubted God would, but none knew how he could, fulfill his promise.

"I've heated the water!"

"No need to yell, Joseph, I hear you fine."

Mary would have heard had Joseph whispered. The stable was even smaller than Joseph had imagined, but the innkeeper was right—it was clean. I started to clear out the sheep and cow, but Michael stopped me. "The Father wants all of creation to witness the moment."

Mary cried out and gripped Joseph's arm with one hand and a feed trough with the other. The thrust in her abdomen lifted her back, and she leaned forward.

"Is it time?" Joseph asked.

She shot back a glance, and he had his answer.

Within moments the Awaited One was born. I was

privileged to have a position close to the couple, only a step behind Michael. We both gazed into the wrinkled face of the infant. Joseph had placed hay in a feed trough, giving Jesus his first bed.

All of God was in the infant. Light encircled his face and radiated from his tiny hands. The very glory I had witnessed in his throne room now burst through his skin.

I felt we should sing but did not know what. We had no song. We had no verse. We had never seen the sight of God in a baby. When God had made a star, our words had roared. When he had delivered his servants, our tongues had flown with praise. Before his throne, our songs never ended. But what do you sing to God in a feed trough?

In that moment a wonderful thing happened. As we looked at the baby Jesus, the darkness lifted. Not the darkness of the night, but the darkness of the mystery. Heaven's enlightenment engulfed the legions.

Our minds were filled with Truth we had never before known. We became aware for the first time of the Father's plan to rescue those who bear his name. He revealed to us all that was to come. At once amazed and stunned, the eye of every angel went to one part of the child: the hands that would be pierced. "At the pounding of the nail," God told us, "you will not save him. You will watch, you will hear, you will yearn, but you will not rescue."

Paragon and Aegus turned to me, begging for an explanation. I had none. *I exist to serve my King, and I must watch him be tortured?* I looked to Michael; his face was stone-hard with torment. I recognized the look, for I felt the same. We could not fathom the command. "How will we sit silent as you suffer?" we asked in unison.

There was no response.

Sophio was whispering. I drew near to hear his words:

"A child has been given to us; God has given a Son to us. He will be responsible for leading the people. His name will be:

Wonderful Counselor,

Powerful God,

Father Who Lives Forever,

Prince of Peace.

He will be wounded for the wrong they did, crushed for the evil they did. The punishment that will make them well will be given to him. They will be healed because of his wounds."

Once again, I heard the words I had heard first in the throne room. Only this time, I understood.

So this is he. Immanuel. So this is God's gift. A Savior. He shall save his people from their sins. "Worthy is the Lamb," I whispered as I knelt before my God. My heart was full. I turned to Mary as she cradled her child and I spoke. It didn't matter that she couldn't hear me. The stars could. All of nature could. And most of all, my King could.

"Do you know who you hold, Mary? You secure the Author of grace. He who is ageless is now moments old. He who is limitless is now suckling your milk. He who strides upon the stars, now has legs too weak to walk; the hands that held the oceans are now an infant's fist. To him who has never asked a question, you will teach the name of the wind. The source of language will learn words from you. He who has never stumbled, you will carry. He who has never hungered, you will feed. The King of creation is in your arms."

"What manner of love is this?" Michael whispered, and again we were covered with silence. A blanket of awe. Finally, Michael again opened his mouth, this time to sing. He began quietly, pausing between the words. "Glory, glory, glory to God in the highest."

One by one we joined in. "Glory, glory, glory to God in the highest."

Gradually the chorus grew louder and faster: "Glory, glory to God in the highest. Glory, glory to God in the highest. Glory, glory to God in the highest."

Our praise rose into the realms of the universe. In the most distant galaxy the dust on the oldest star danced with our praise. In the depths of the ocean, the water rippled with adoration. The tiniest microbe turned, the mightiest constellation spun, all of nature joined with us as we worshiped Immanuel, the God who had become flesh.

The babe of Bethlehem. Immanuel. Remember the promise of the angel? "'Behold, the virgin shall be with child, and bear a Son, and they shall call His name Immanuel,' which is translated, 'God with us'" (Matt. 1:23 NKJV).

Immanuel. The name appears in the same Hebrew form as it did two thousand years ago. "Immanu" means "with us." "El" refers to Elohim, or God. Not an "above us God" or a "somewhere in the neighborhood God." He came as the "with us God." God with us.

Not "God with the rich" or "God with the religious." But God with *us*. All of us. Russians, Germans, Buddhists, Mormons, truckdrivers and taxi drivers, librarians. God with *us*.

Cure for the Common Life

Tiny Mouth, Tiny Feet

*T*he stable stinks like all stables do. The stench of urine, dung, and sheep reeks pungently in the air. The ground is hard, the hay scarce. Cobwebs cling to the ceiling, and a mouse scurries across the dirt floor.

A more lowly place of birth could not exist.

Off to one side sit a group of shepherds. They sit silently on the floor; perhaps perplexed, perhaps in awe, no doubt in amazement. Their night watch had been interrupted by an explosion of light from heaven and a symphony of angels. God goes to those who have time to hear him—so on this cloudless night he went to simple shepherds.

Near the young mother sits the weary father. If anyone is dozing, he is. He can't remember the last time he sat down. And now that the excitement has subsided a bit, now that Mary and the baby are comfortable, he leans against the wall of the stable and feels his eyes grow heavy. He still hasn't figured it all out. The mystery of the event puzzles him. But he hasn't the energy to wrestle with the questions. What's important is that the baby is fine and that Mary is safe. As sleep comes, he remembers the name the angel told him to use . . . Jesus. "We will call him Jesus."

Wide awake is Mary. My, how young she looks! Her head rests on the soft leather of Joseph's saddle. The pain has been eclipsed by wonder. She looks into the face of the baby. Her son. Her Lord. His Majesty. At this point in history, the human being who best understands who God is and what he is doing is a teenage girl in a smelly stable. She can't take her eyes off him. Somehow Mary knows she is holding God. So this is he. She remembers the words of the angel. "His kingdom will never end" (Luke 1:33 NIV).

He looks like anything but a king. His face is prunish and red. His cry, though strong and healthy, is still the helpless and piercing cry of a baby. And he is absolutely dependent upon Mary for his well-being.

Majesty in the midst of the mundane. Holiness in the filth of sheep manure and sweat. Divinity entering the world on the floor of a stable, through the womb of a teenager and in the presence of a carpenter.

She touches the face of the infant-God. *How long was your journey!*

This baby had overlooked the universe. These rags keeping him warm were the robes of eternity. His golden throne room had been abandoned in favor of a dirty sheep pen.

And so she prays . . .

God. O infant-God. Heaven's fairest child. Conceived by the union of divine grace with our disgrace. Sleep well.

Sleep well. Bask in the coolness of this night bright with diamonds. Sleep well, for the heat of anger simmers nearby. Enjoy the silence of the crib, for the noise of confusion rumbles in your future. Savor the sweet safety of my arms, for a day is soon coming when I cannot protect you.

Rest well, tiny hands. For though you belong to a king, you will touch no satin, own no gold. You will grasp no pen, guide no brush. No, your tiny hands are reserved for works more precious:

> to touch a leper's open wound,
> to wipe a widow's weary tear,
> to claw the ground of Gethsemane.

Your hands, so tiny, so tender, so white—clutched tonight in an infant's fist. They aren't destined to hold a scepter nor wave from a palace balcony. They are reserved instead for a Roman spike that will staple them to a Roman cross.

Sleep deeply, tiny eyes. Sleep while you can. For soon the blurriness will clear, and you will see the mess we have made of your world.

> You will see our nakedness, for we cannot hide.
> You will see our selfishness, for we cannot give.
> You will see our pain, for we cannot heal.

O eyes that will see hell's darkest pit and witness her ugly prince . . . sleep, please sleep; sleep while you can.

Lay still, tiny mouth. Lay still mouth from which eternity will speak.

Tiny tongue that will soon summon the dead,
that will define grace,
that will silence our foolishness.

Rosebud lips—upon which ride a starborn kiss of forgiveness to those who believe you and of death to those who deny you—lay still.

And tiny feet cupped in the palm of my hand, rest. For many difficult steps lie ahead for you . . .

Do you feel the cold seawater upon which you will walk?

Do you wrench at the invasion of the nail you will bear?

Do you fear the steep descent down the spiral staircase into Satan's domain?

Rest, tiny feet. Rest today so that tomorrow you might walk with power. Rest. For millions will follow in your steps.

And little heart . . . holy heart . . . pumping the blood of life through the universe: How many times will we break you?

You'll be torn by the thorns of our accusations.
You'll be ravaged by the cancer of our sin.
You'll be crushed under the weight of your own
    sorrow.
And you'll be pierced by the spear of our rejection.

Yet in that piercing, in that ultimate ripping of muscle and membrane, in that final rush of blood and water, you will find rest. Your hands will be freed, your eyes will see justice, your lips will smile, and your feet will carry you home.

And there you'll rest again—this time in the embrace of your Father.

GOD CAME NEAR

I Love Christmas

I love Christmas. Let the sleigh bells ring. Let the carolers sing. The more Santas the merrier. The more trees the better.

I love Christmas. The ho ho ho, the rooty toot toot, the thumpety, thump, thump, and the pa rum pa pum pum. The "Silent Night" and the sugarplums.

I don't complain about the crowded shops. I don't grumble at the jam-packed grocery store. The flight is full? The restaurant is packed? Well, it's Christmas.

And I love Christmas.

Bring on Scrooge, Cousin Eddie, and the "official

Red Ryder, carbine-action, two-hundred shot range model air rifle." "You'll shoot your eye out!"

The tinsel and the clatter and waking up "to see what was the matter." Bing and his tunes. Macy's balloons. Mistletoe kisses, Santa Claus wishes, and favorite dishes. Holiday snows, warm winter clothes, and Rudolph's red nose.

I love Christmas.

I love it because somewhere someone will ask the Christmas questions: What's the big deal about the baby in the manger? Who was he? What does his birth have to do with me? The questioner may be a child looking at a front-yard crèche. He may be a soldier stationed far from home. She may be a young mom who, for the first time, holds a child on Christmas Eve. The Christmas season prompts questions.

I can remember the first time I asked those questions. I grew up in a small West Texas town, the son of a mechanic and a nurse. Never poor but certainly not affluent. My dad laid pipeline in the oil fields. Mom worked the three-to-eleven shift at the hospital. I followed my brother to elementary school every morning and played neighborhood ball in the afternoons.

Dad was in charge of dinner. My brother washed the dishes, and I was in charge of sweeping the floor. We boys took our baths by eight and were in bed by nine with permission to do one thing before turning out the lights. We could read.

The chest at the foot of our bed contained children's books. Big books, each with a glossy finish and bright pictures. The three bears lived in the chest. So did the big, bad wolf and seven dwarfs and a monkey with a lunch pail, whose name I don't recall. Somewhere in the chest, beneath the fairy tales, was a book about baby Jesus.

On the cover was a yellow-hayed manger. A star glowed above the stable. Joseph and a donkey, equally big eyed, stood nearby. Mary held a baby in her arms. She looked down at him, and he looked up at her, and I remember looking at them both.

My dad, a man of few words, had told my brother and me, "Boys, Christmas is about Christ."

In one of those bedtime, book-time moments, somewhere between the fairy tales and the monkey with the lunch pail, I thought about what he had said. I began asking the Christmas questions. In one way or another, I've been asking them ever since.

I love the answers I have found.

Like this one: God knows what it is like to be a human. When I talk to him about deadlines or long lines or tough times, he understands. He's been there. He's been *here*. Because of Bethlehem, I have a friend in heaven.

Because of Bethlehem, I have a Savior in heaven. Christmas begins what Easter celebrates. The child in the cradle became the King on the cross. And because he did, there are no marks on my record. Just grace. His offer has no fine print.

He didn't tell me, "Clean up before you come in." He offered, "Come in and I'll clean you up." It's not my grip on him that matters but his grip on me. And his grip is sure.

So is his presence in my life. Christmas presents from Santa? That's nice. But the perpetual presence of Christ? That's life changing.

God is always near us. Always for us. Always in us. We may forget him, but God will never forget us. We are forever on his mind and in his plans. He called himself "'Immanuel' (which means 'God with us')" (Matt. 1:23).

Not just "God made us."

Not just "God thinks of us."

Not just "God above us."

But God *with* us. God where we are: at the office, in the kitchen, on the plane. He breathed our air and walked this earth. God . . . with . . . us!

We need this message more than ever. We live in anxious times. Terrorism is living up to its name—terror. Violence hangs over our planet like a dark cloud. Think about the images on the news: the senseless attacks, the bloodshed, the random acts of cruelty.

And, as if the malice were inadequate, there is the fear of another recession. We seem to teeter on the edge of bull markets going bear and the financial world going down. The shepherds stayed awake, watching their flocks by night. You've been sleeping with one eye open trying to keep watch over your stocks by night.

And there is more:

The job you can't keep

The tumor you can't diagnose

The marriage you can't fix

The boss you can't please

We can relate to the little boy who played the part of the angel in the Christmas story. He and his mother rehearsed his lines over and over: "It is I; don't be afraid." "It is I; don't be afraid."

Yet, when the Christmas pageant began, he walked onto the stage and saw the lights and audience and he froze. After an awkward silence, he finally said, "It is me and I'm scared."

Are you scared? If so, may I suggest that you need a little Christmas? I don't mean a dose of saccharine sentiment or Santa cheer or double-spiked eggnog. That's not Christmas.

Christmas, as my dad said, is about Christ. Christ's name occupies six of the nine letters, for crying out loud. This isn't Santa-mas, or shopping-mas, or reindeer-mas. This is *Christ*-mas. And *Christ*-mas is not *Christ*-mas unless or until you receive the message of Bethlehem.

Have you? In the hurry and scurry of the season, have you taken time to receive the promise of the season?

God gets us.
God saves us.

God is always near us. By the way, Bethlehem was just the beginning. Jesus has promised a repeat performance. Bethlehem, Act 2. No silent night this time, however. The skies will open, trumpets will blast, and a new kingdom will begin. He will empty the tombs and melt the winter of death. He will press his thumb against the collective cheek of his children and wipe away all tears. "Begone, sorrow, sickness, wheelchairs, and cancer! Enough of you, screams of fear and nights of horror! Death, you die! Life, you reign!" The manger invites, even dares us to believe the best is yet to be. And it could all begin today.

But if it doesn't, there is a reason. No day is accidental or incidental. No acts are random or wasted. Look at the Bethlehem birth. A king ordered a census. Joseph was forced to travel. Mary, as round as a ladybug, bounced on a donkey's back. The hotel was full. The hour was late. The event was one big hassle. Yet, out of the hassle, hope was born.

It still is. I don't like hassles. But I love Christmas because it reminds us how "God causes everything to work together for the good of those who love God" (Rom. 8:28 NLT).

The heart-shaping promises of Christmas. Long after the guests have left and the carolers have gone home and the lights have come down, these promises endure.

Perhaps you could use some Christmas this Christmas? Let's do what I did as a six-year-old, red-headed, flat- topped, freckle-faced boy. Let's turn on the lamp, curl up in a comfortable spot, and look into the odd, wonderful story of Bethlehem.

May you find what I have found: a lifetime of hope.

Because of Bethlehem

SOURCES

S ome of the material in this book was originally published in the following books by Max Lucado. All copyrights to the original works are held by the author, Max Lucado.

3:16: Numbers of Hope (Nashville: Thomas Nelson, 2007).

And the Angels Were Silent (Nashville: Thomas Nelson, 2003).

The Applause of Heaven (Nashville: Thomas Nelson, 1990).

Because of Bethlehem (Nashville: Thomas Nelson, 2016)

Cure for the Common Life (Nashville: Thomas Nelson, 2005).

A Gentle Thunder (Nashville: Thomas Nelson, 1995).

God Came Near (Nashville: Thomas Nelson, 2003).

He Chose the Nails (Nashville: Thomas Nelson, 2000).

He Still Moves Stones (Nashville: Thomas Nelson, 1993).

In the Grip of Grace (Nashville: Thomas Nelson, 1996).

A Love Worth Giving (Nashville: Thomas Nelson, 2002).

Next Door Savior (Nashville: Thomas Nelson, 2003).

When God Whispers Your Name (Nashville: Thomas Nelson, 1994).

ABOUT THE AUTHOR

www.karenjames.com

*S*ince entering the ministry in 1978, Max Lucado has served churches in Miami, Florida; Rio de Janeiro, Brazil; and San Antonio, Texas. He currently serves as Teaching Minister of Oak Hills Church in San Antonio. He is the recipient of the 2021 ECPA Pinnacle Award for his outstanding contribution to the publishing industry and society at large. He is America's bestselling inspirational author with more than 145 million products in print.

Visit his website at MaxLucado.com
Facebook.com/MaxLucado
Instagram.com/MaxLucado
Twitter.com/MaxLucado